# Do You Believe In Santa?

## SIERRA DONOVAN

**ZEBRA BOOKS**
**KENSINGTON PUBLISHING CORP.**
http://www.kensingtonbooks.com

ZEBRA BOOKS are published by

Kensington Publishing Corp.
119 West 40th Street
New York, NY 10018

All Kensington titles, imprints, and distributed lines are available at special quantity discounts for bulk purchases for sales promotion, premiums, fund-raising, educational, or institutional use.

Special book excerpts or customized printings can also be created to fit specific needs. For details, write or phone the office of the Kensington Sales Manager: Attn.: Sales Department. Kensington Publishing Corp., 119 West 40th Street, New York, NY 10018. Phone: 1-800-221-2647.

First Printing: October 2015
ISBN-13: 978-1-4201-3422-3
ISBN-10: 1-4201-3422-1

eISBN-13: 978-1-4201-3423-0
eISBN-10: 1-4201-3423-X

10 9 8 7 6 5 4 3 2 1

Printed in the United States of America

# IF YOU BELIEVE

Mandy's voice stood out to Jake above the others, not just because she was standing next to him, and not because her voice was better than anyone else's, although it did have a sweet timbre. Just because it was Mandy's.

Jake looked down at her, and the glow on her face was more than the soft, colored light cast by the tree. It was a look of pure joy and contentment. *She does this every year,* he thought. *And every year, she loves it just as much.*

Was it because she'd lived her entire life in the same town and didn't have anything to compare it to? If that were the case, you'd think the brightness in her eyes would have gotten dimmer by now. She'd stayed in Tall Pine, taken a ton of ribbing about her vision of Santa Claus, and still she glowed. Maybe that was because this was where she truly belonged. Maybe Mandy's roots in this town ran as deep as the roots of the Tall Pine tree.

Up to now, Jake reflected, he'd been content to move from place to place. It had been convenient, he supposed, to avoid any reminders of past mistakes, to start over again in a new place and make a fresh impression.

Maybe it was time for him to put down some roots, too . . .

**Books by Sierra Donovan**

NO CHRISTMAS LIKE THE PRESENT

DO YOU BELIEVE IN SANTA?

**Published by Kensington Publishing Corporation**

*To Mom, who taught me to believe in Santa*

*Christmas spirit is about believing, not seeing.*
—Santa Claus, *Elf*


*Now faith is the substance of things hoped for, the evidence of things not seen.*
—Hebrews 11:1

# Prologue

*When Mandy Reese was eight years old, she saw Santa Claus.*

*She slipped out of her room on Christmas Eve after her mother went to bed. As Mandy tiptoed down the hall, trying to be silent, she thought of the poem:* Not a creature was stirring, not even a mouse. . . .

*The Christmas tree was still lit up in the living room, as if it, too, were waiting. The nighttime cold of the house bit through her flannel nightgown, and Mandy wished she'd grabbed her robe and slippers. But she didn't want to risk going back down the hall and waking her mother. So she pulled a heavy blanket down from the back of the sofa and curled up under it. She laid her head on the arm of the couch to get a good view of the tree at the end of the room near her head, and the fireplace at the other end, down by her feet.*

*Barely daring to breathe, she waited.*

*The lights from the tree were bright enough to show the time on the clock over the mantel: almost eleven-thirty.*

*Mandy's vigilant eyes drifted from the fireplace to the tree and back. She knew there was no way she'd fall asleep.*

*But it felt as if some time had passed when something made her sit up.*

*The only light in the room still came from the tree, yet somehow it seemed brighter in here. Her eyes darted to the fireplace. And he was there.*

*He did wear a red suit, although it was a darker red than she'd seen on the Santas at the store—the ones she'd always been told were just helpers for the real Santa. His beard was full and white, his eyebrows were bushy, and his eyes were blue. Not quite twinkly, a little more serious than that, but warm and friendly as they met hers. She'd heard that watching for Santa could make him pass you by, but that hint of a glimmer in his eye told her she wasn't in trouble.*

*Mandy opened her mouth to speak, but she couldn't think of a single word to say. The whole room felt hushed, as if time were standing still.*

*She couldn't be dreaming because her heart was beating so fast. But she remembered to pinch her forearm, hard, just to be sure. It hurt, all right.*

*He took a step backward, toward the chimney, and raised a black-gloved finger. At first Mandy thought he was going to put it to his lips, signaling her to be quiet. But he rested it alongside his nose, just like the poem, and nodded.*

*The room brightened, and Mandy had to shut her eyes against the glare.*

*When she opened them, the light in the room had returned to the normal Christmas-tree glow, and he was gone. She heard the clock on the mantel ticking; she didn't remember hearing the sound while Santa was in the room. The hands showed it was just after midnight, although she knew for certain she hadn't heard it chime.*

*She pinched her arm again. Once again, it hurt. When she looked down, she saw a small red mark forming right next to the spot she was pinching now.*

*Under the tree, she couldn't see any difference in the number of presents. But she remembered what her mother always told her: Santa Claus was about more than presents.*

*"I saw him," she whispered.*

When Mandy told her mother about it the next morning, her mom checked the doors and windows and counted the presents under the tree.

"I thought you believed in Santa Claus," Mandy said.

"I do." But the worried look didn't quite go away.

The memory of her mother's reaction kept Mandy from mentioning Santa when school started again in January. If her mom didn't believe her, the other kids surely wouldn't, and Mandy didn't want to fight about it. So she kept it to herself, like her own special secret. Until the next school year.

It was mid-December, and she was leaving school Friday afternoon to catch the bus. There hadn't been any snow for a couple of weeks, but there was a snap to the air as she walked. Mandy was so busy looking up at the sky for signs of snow, she didn't see the crowd outside the gate until she was nearly there.

Students clustered around an auburn-haired woman who held a microphone. A man stood nearby, aiming a video camera at the woman. Then it clicked. Mandy had seen her on the television news.

As the kids crowded around the reporter, she held a microphone in front of some of them, one at a time. Most were younger than Mandy. Older kids jockeyed behind the TV reporter, trying to poke their heads into the picture.

"I believe he's real," a little blond boy, probably a second-grader, said.

"He always eats the cookies we leave for him," a fair-haired girl, who looked like his sister, said.

Mandy joined the group as if drawn by a magnet. Since many of the children were shorter, she could see over their heads.

"What about you?" The reporter aimed her

microphone at a brown-eyed girl with short black hair.

"I don't know." Her voice was very soft. "I think so."

"I used to believe in Santa, but I know better now." That was Julie Ashman, from Mandy's own class. Mandy felt her blood start to simmer. Being wrong was one thing, but saying things like that in front of these little kids . . .

"Santa Claus is a fake!" one of the taller boys behind the reporter shouted toward the microphone.

"No, he's not!" The little blond boy looked faintly horrified, and Mandy could see uncertainty creeping into his face.

The reporter tried to regain control, turning her microphone toward the smaller boy again.

"Oh, yeah?" the big boy jeered. "Have you ever seen him? Not in a store. That doesn't count."

She couldn't stand it. Mandy shouldered her way in. "*I* saw him."

Everyone turned in her direction. Mandy's face felt hot, but she was determined to set them straight. "He was at my house."

"Not your dad, all dressed up," the older boy scoffed.

"My dad doesn't live with us anymore," Mandy said, "and I saw Santa Claus in my living room last year."

Suddenly the microphone and the camera were pointed at her, and Mandy felt the words rush out, spilling the details she'd played over and over in her mind. The story she'd kept bottled up for nearly a year.

# Chapter 1

"Then he laid a finger aside his nose . . ." Mandy told the wide-eyed four-year-old boy.

From her crouched position, she glanced past the brown-haired boy's shoulder for just a moment. His mother, standing behind him in the little shop, was smiling with a touch of the Christmas glimmer in her eyes, even though it was the middle of August.

". . . and, *whoosh!* He went right up the chimney."

"Did he drop anything?"

About half of the children asked her that.

"Nope. He was very careful."

"Did he bring you what you wanted for Christmas?"

A lot of them asked her that, too.

"There were a lot of presents under the tree," Mandy said carefully, glancing past the boy at his mother again. "But after he left, I couldn't even remember what I wanted that year. You know why?"

"Why?"

"Because seeing Santa was the best Christmas present I ever got."

Mandy straightened, smiling at them both. She didn't often have the chance to tell the story in the heart of summer; this visit was a treat. One of the nearby store owners must have sent them over.

"Did you ever see—?"

"Robbie." The little boy's mother patted his shoulder. "We've taken up enough of this lady's time." She met Mandy's eyes. "Thank you. We'll take these."

The woman handed Mandy a pair of peppermint-striped salt and pepper shakers, and Mandy took them behind the counter to the cash register. "I love these. I have a set at home."

As Mandy wrapped the shakers in tissue paper, Robbie's mother fished in her purse for her wallet, still glancing over the necklaces, key chains and other Christmas knickknacks displayed on the countertop. "It must be hard not to take the whole store home with you."

"Oh, I think I already have." Mandy grinned as she rang up the sale.

The North Pole was the kind of store that wouldn't stand much of a chance outside of a mountain town: ninety percent Christmas merchandise. But when visitors to Tall Pine wandered the shops on Evergreen Lane, most of them stepped inside for a quick look, and many left with a knickknack or two. Mandy thought it might be something about the mountain air and the scent of pine that helped people catch the Christmas spirit, even in the off-season.

As Mandy handed the customer her bag, Robbie said, "Hey, that's you! Are you famous?"

He was pointing at the two framed newspaper clippings on the south wall. One was the original story the paper had run the year Mandy told the television reporter about Santa Claus. The other was from six years back: *SANTA SIGHTER GOES TO WORK AT CHRISTMAS STORE.* The photo showed an eighteen-year-old Mandy standing in nearly the same spot she was right now, smiling behind the counter. She didn't know if anyone else could see the slight discomfort beneath the smile.

"No, I'm not famous," she said, feeling a trace of a blush warm her cheeks. "They just wrote a couple of stories about me. Because not everyone gets to see Santa."

The framed clippings were the only part of the job Mandy didn't care for, but it was the reason Mrs. Swanson had hired her. And Mandy had wanted, with all her heart, to work at The North Pole. It was filled with the things she loved, and she loved telling her story to the kids who occasionally came in to hear it. The clippings reminded her of the hard part, the kidding she'd taken all through school. But if it meant being here every day to share the magic, then so be it.

Robbie took his mother's hand as she led him toward the door.

"Hey." Mandy reached into the crystal bowl on the countertop. "Want a candy cane for the road?"

"A candy cane? In the summer?"

"Sure, why not? They're still fresh, I promise." Mandy winked at him. "I had one earlier this morning."

Mother and son stepped forward, and each of them took one of the short, cellophane-wrapped candies.

"Merry Christmas," she said.

The little boy waved, and the sleigh bells hanging from the door jingled behind them as they left.


Jake Wyndham strolled the sidewalk of Evergreen Lane, peering in the occasional window. He'd already checked out a T-shirt store and a sporting goods shop. He'd looked over the menu posted in the window of a sandwich shop, but it was too early for lunch. The street had a lot of foot traffic, a healthy sign on a Saturday morning. So far, everything he saw supported his company's research: Tall Pine looked like a town that drew a fair number of weekend visitors.

Up ahead, two red-and-white-striped poles

supported the awning over the entrance to another store. It didn't quite look like a barber shop. . . . No, wait, those were supposed to be big peppermint sticks.

Jake got close enough to see the display in the nearest of the two windows flanking the entrance to the store. The large sill was decked in cotton that passed for snow, with a miniature Christmas village laid out on top. Tiny children on little toboggans pretended to slide down an improvised hill.

The red letters on the shop window read THE NORTH POLE.

Okay, this could be interesting.

He pulled open the door, to be greeted by the jingling of the bells that hung on it. From speakers overhead, Jake recognized a voice that he never heard any time of year but December: Bing Crosby.

*"May your days be merry and bright. . . ."*

They weren't kidding around about this. Reindeer, snowmen and nutcrackers filled the shop: figurines on shelves, pictures and plaques on the walls, jewelry and key chains hanging from display hooks in front of the counter. Artificial Christmas trees, large and small, poked up from corners and alongside rows of shelves, decorated with price-tagged ornaments. It was a world of red and green, peppermint and pine. Jake had never seen anything like it back home in Scranton, that was for sure.

He stepped slowly forward, the old tenet of "you break it, you bought it" echoing in his head. Thankfully, the rows of shelves weren't so close together that bumping into them was a hazard. What had felt like a manic clutter at first glance was actually arranged rather nicely. A cluster of mugs here, candleholders there . . . and, Jake was astonished to see, a whole shelf devoted to salt and pepper shakers. Did people really—

"Hi."

Jake turned to see a pretty, dark-haired woman step from behind one of the Christmas trees a few feet to his left. "Can I help you find anything?" she added.

"Not at the moment."

She had a warm, ready smile, and her eyes were a deep blue. She held an ornament that looked like a little wooden rowboat. Jake's eyes went from the ornament to the tree, and he saw it was decorated with other outdoorsy items: elk, geese, pinecones, even a snowman with a fishing pole.

"I see you're going with a theme," he said.

"It's fun." The girl hung the boat on a branch and reached into a box resting on a nearby stool. She fished out another ornament—appropriately enough, a fish. "I could never stick to one thing on my tree at home. There are so many personal memories that go with Christmas decorations. But it's fun to do it here."

Jake watched deft fingers with unpainted nails hang up a dark-furred grizzly bear. "How does your store do when it's not Christmastime? Is it pretty slow?"

"Oh, it's quieter, for sure." She gestured around the store, empty of any other customers, with a little shrug. "But people trickle in. And when they do, they usually buy something."

"Locals? Or tourists?"

"I guess you'd say local tourists. People from maybe an hour or two away. During the summer they like to come up for the day because it's cooler up here in the mountains. And in the winter it gets pretty crazy. We're the first town people hit when they drive up to go to the snow."

"'Go to the snow'?"

"Sure. Down the hill, it never snows. You usually have to be at least four thousand feet up to get snow in Southern California." She studied him with a quizzical frown.

He stepped back, feeling as if he'd been found out. "Sorry, I'm from Pennsylvania. The idea of driving somewhere to *visit* snow never occurred to me."

She grinned. "I guess so. If you never get snow, it's a novelty. Up here we have to dig our way out of it sometimes. But it's so beautiful."

She looked almost starry-eyed. Clearly, she hadn't

**13**

gotten over the novelty of snow. "Have you lived here long?" he asked.

"All my life." She picked up the box and stepped back to view her handiwork. It brought her one step closer to Jake, and he sneaked a look at her contemplative profile. Her blue eyes had a soulful look he couldn't remember seeing on any adult.

He took his eyes from her face before she caught him staring, and noticed a silver bell earring dangling from her earlobe.

*Silver bells . . . Oh. Right. Got it.*

Apparently satisfied with the tree, she walked past him with a smile, taking the box behind the counter and setting it down. "So," she said, "what brings you here from Pennsylvania?"

"Do you have anything for a seven-year-old girl? My niece," he added, not sure why he felt the urge to clarify.

Her eyes went ceilingward as she contemplated the problem.

The reason he'd come to town wouldn't be a secret for long, but Jake found he usually got better answers to his questions if people didn't know why he was asking. Regal Hotels had sent him to set up their next location, and the demographics of Tall Pine looked great. But getting the perspective of locals often came in handy.

The woman's eyes roamed over the store. "Really, just about anything, except maybe for the glass breakables," she said. "Are you looking for something a little less seasonal? For a souvenir?"

Jake nodded. "Exactly."

"Does she like jewelry?"

He hesitated.

"Oh, I don't mean diamonds and rubies." That smile reached her eyes every time. "Just a little bauble."

Bauble?

She reached over to a display rack of necklaces on the countertop, turning it to show the different designs. Bears, Santa hats, Christmas trees . . . Her fingers came to rest, cupping a tiny pinecone about the size of a thimble. His niece, Emily, *would* like that.

"We sell a lot of these," she said. "They're real pinecones, but they're treated with lacquer so they'll last. Pinecone . . . Tall Pine?"

*Got it.* Jake eyed the price tag on the chain: ten dollars. "That's perfect. Thanks."

She wrapped the necklace in tissue paper as gently as if it were a crystal vase. Meanwhile, Jake became aware of the music from the speakers again. It had left Bing Crosby and moved on to Nat King Cole. "Do you ever get tired of Christmas music?"

"You'd be surprised how often people ask me that." *Not really.* "But I never do. There's so much good Christmas music. I bring a lot of it from home."

She rang up the necklace and handed him the bag, silver bells glinting below her ears. "Merry Christmas."

"Merry Christmas," he said before he thought. With Nat King Cole in the background, it came as a reflex.

He walked out the door, bells jingling behind him. The warm summer day came as a shock after being surrounded by mistletoe and holly.

An unexpected voice piped up in his head, as if it were chiming in with the bells: *You should have asked her out.*

The multipaned door swung shut. Too late.

Besides, he had work to do, and he knew where to find her.

Resisting the urge to look back through the glass, Jake set off to continue his fact-finding foray up the street.

# Chapter 2

"Did I miss anything?"

Mrs. Swanson came into the store about half an hour after Mandy's tall, brown-eyed customer left. The shop owner stowed her purse and sunglasses on a shelf behind the counter.

"Not too much." Mandy set down the reindeer figurine she was dusting. One down, seven to go. "We sold one of those beautiful Jim Shore figures, some salt and pepper shakers, and a pinecone necklace. And I got to tell a little boy about Santa."

Mrs. Swanson nodded her satisfaction. She'd never been one to lay on the compliments—not even, from what Mandy heard, to the third-graders she'd taught before she retired. Mandy hadn't even been in her class, and she still never called her anything but Mrs. Swanson. The older woman's appearance never seemed to change: always the same dark gray hair, just a shade away from brunette, worn in the same carefully ordered waves.

She still didn't miss anything, either. She crossed the store to appraise the tree Mandy had just finished decorating. It met with the same brief nod of approval. Coming from Mrs. Swanson, that was as good as an A.

"I'll bring some more things out for the fall table after lunch," Mandy said.

To the right of the register stood the table they used for merchandise to fit the current season, or the one just ahead. It offered a few more choices for people who weren't in the market for Christmas merchandise just yet. Right now it was decked with pumpkins and scarecrows displayed on small bales of hay.

Mandy's handsome customer hadn't wandered over to that side of the shop, or he might have spotted the newspaper clippings on the south wall.

"Did you leave anything for me to do?" Mrs. Swanson said.

Mandy grinned. "There's always the dusting." But she didn't quite have the nerve to hand Mrs. Swanson the feather duster.

Walking behind the counter, Mandy set the duster on a shelf and grabbed her purse. "Guess I'll go to lunch."

If she knew Mrs. Swanson, some dusting would get done. But the owner's primary task these days was to fill in when Mandy was off duty. It was a pretty effective two-woman operation, except for the holiday season, when they hired extra help.

"Don't be long," Mrs. Swanson said, straight-faced. "I don't know if I can handle this rush all by myself."

Most days, Mandy brought her own lunch and ate it in the back room, but today she felt like getting out.

She stepped onto the sidewalk and breathed in the evergreen scent that Tall Pine was blessed with all year round. Most people who lived here said they stopped smelling it after a while, but Mandy never did, and she never got tired of it.

Not sure what she was hungry for, she turned to the right of the store, where most of the restaurants were located. As she approached the Pine 'n' Dine, she noticed a familiar-looking man seated at a table near the black wrought-iron fence that enclosed the restaurant's patio. Thick brown hair, light blue polo shirt, khaki slacks . . . and a folded bag from The North Pole on the table in front of him. Yep. It was the man who'd just bought the pinecone necklace.

He was facing the street corner just past the cafe, his left side to the street, giving Mandy a view of his profile. He leaned slightly back in his chair, a large tablet of paper resting on his knee. A pen or pencil moved over the page, and as she got closer, Mandy made out a studious expression on his face. Sketching? Curious, she stepped closer to the wrought-iron fence, trying to sneak a glimpse.

Instead of a drawing, she saw a lined sheet with columns of handwritten figures.

*Numbers,* she thought. Disappointed, she started to sidle away, but her shoe scraped on the gravel, and he turned in her direction.

The slight furrow disappeared from his brow, and a wide smile crossed his face. "Hey, it's the Christmas girl."

His quick transformation caught Mandy off guard. "That's what they call me."

"Always?" As she fumbled for a response, he prodded, "You must have a name."

"Mandy." She smiled. "Mandy Reese."

"Jake Wyndham." Straightening in his chair, he held out a hand to her over the bars of the little fence. "It's nice to run into you again."

She took his hand and felt her smile get bigger. "Long time no see."

Brown eyes met hers with a steady, perceptive look. No wonder she'd pegged him for an artist, instead of an accountant or whatever he was. Mandy fought off a sense of self-consciousness.

Jake released her hand and shifted in his chair. "So, help me out." With his pencil, he tapped the menu on the table in front of him. "I haven't ordered yet. What's good here?"

That was easy. "I love the Chinese chicken salad."

He nodded. "Do you have a second choice, keeping in mind that I'm a guy?"

Mandy fumbled for a response. Was he flirting with her? It wasn't like she had a lot of practice, so it was hard to tell. The local men her own age were all the same ones who'd teased her in school, and the clientele at The North Pole wasn't heavily male. Last summer a customer had asked her out, but she didn't think one sixteen-year-old blond surfer dude really counted. *Mandy Reese. Twenty-four-year-old cougar.*

"I don't suppose you'd care to join me?" he asked.

Her heart thumped. Maybe he was flirting, or maybe he was just being friendly. Either way, she didn't take long to debate her answer. "Sure."

Mandy circled to the restaurant's entrance to join him. Didn't he know she hadn't even gone to her prom? Of course he didn't. Not that this was anything like prom. Just a friendly lunch, not exactly a date.

After they ordered, Mandy nodded toward the tablet Jake had stashed on the unoccupied chair at his right. "So, what's with all the numbers?"

"Well, here's the deal." Jake glanced at the pad

of figures. "I work for Regal Hotels. It's a national chain. Have you heard of it?"

She recognized the name from television commercials. Mandy nodded.

"They sent me to see about opening a new location out here. Sometimes things look good on paper, but you can't be sure until you come up and see a place." He nodded at the pad on the chair, like a third party at their lunch. "So far it feels great. This is a really nice little town."

He looked at her as if he were paying her a personal compliment. When Mandy didn't respond, he went on.

"So for starters, I come up here, talk to some people, crunch some numbers. Get a feel for the population, how much tourist traffic there is, cost of putting in a location. That's step one. If everything looks good, I start working with city officials, checking into land availability, permits, that kind of thing."

"Oh." So their little chat was actually a fact-finding mission. Mandy looked at the tablet again. She decided she didn't much care for the uninvited guest on the chair between them.

Something else about his mission niggled, and she wasn't sure what it was.

"Tall Pine is more than numbers," she heard herself say.

"Of course it is." His brown eyes took on a puzzled look. "That's why I'm here."

Their waitress arrived with their drinks—a Coke for Jake, iced tea for Mandy. The interruption gave Mandy a chance to remember that he was just doing his job. She plucked the slice of lemon from the edge of her glass and adjusted her expectations, officially filing this lunch under *not-a-date*.

"You say you've lived here your whole life?" he asked when the waitress left.

She nodded.

He rested his chin on his folded hands. "And you don't like the idea of someone coming here and sizing up your town."

"I guess that's it." She stirred her tea. "Sorry. Nothing personal."

"Don't be sorry. It's your home." Jake contemplated her. "It's smaller than the other areas I've worked in," he said. "We've been in the major cities for a long time, and a whole lot of the suburbs too. The thinking is, when we branch out to nice tourist towns like this one, customers can find a place to stay that's consistent. We're not fancy, but we're dependable. People know what to expect from a national chain."

*That* was the problem.

"You're going to have a hard time here," she said.

"How so?"

"You're talking about a national chain. Look around you."

**23**

Jake obliged, casting his gaze up and down the sun-dappled street.

"Do you see any fast-food franchises? Chain department stores? Even our grocery store is mom-and-pop."

"And I'll bet you pay higher prices because of that."

"Maybe." She shrugged. "The nearest town is Rolling Hills, and they don't have a chain grocery either. I'd say the nearest one is an hour away, so I don't go comparison shopping. Some people go down the hill to buy their groceries once a week, or a couple times a month—"

"And the town loses business that way."

Mandy bit her lip.

He leaned forward. "You see, once a Regal Hotel opened up here, there'd be more jobs. More shoppers. More money would stay up here, because you'd have more customers for your stores."

She couldn't argue with that. But—"You're missing the point." She gestured out toward the sidewalk. "It's deliberate. They've made it a point to keep big nationwide businesses out of Tall Pine. So it doesn't look like every other town in America. It has its own personality. Its own—"

"Character." He nodded. "I get what you're saying. But if you weigh the benefits—"

He was back to ledger sheets again. She held up

her hands. "Remember, it's not me you need to convince."

"But it's a lot of people who feel the same way you do." He didn't seem particularly wounded. In fact, he smiled. "A small army of Mandys."

She felt the corners of her mouth tug up. "Makes me sound kind of dangerous."

"Oh, I can think of worse things."

Their food arrived. At a loss, Mandy jabbed at her Chinese chicken salad. Here she was, across the table from a nice-looking man who seemed like a decent person, and she was arguing with him. And he was being so calm and reasonable she had no right to get mad at him.

"Hey," he said when they'd been eating in silence for a minute or so.

Mandy looked up. His eyes were serious now. She couldn't remember the last time anyone had looked at her so directly. Why did he have to be talking about hotels, for heaven's sake?

"Thanks for being honest. You've given me an idea what I'll be going up against, and I understand." His eyes wouldn't let her go. "But I want you to know—I'm not here to ruin any of this. I meant what I said. I've just been here a few hours, and I really like it. I won't be bringing in bulldozers towing in half a dozen McDonald's or what-have-you. It's just one hotel."

"But as soon as there's one chain outfit, it

opens the door for more. That's the way the town council's going to see it."

He nodded, and they finished their lunch.

When the waitress brought their bill, Mandy reached across the table for it. "How much do I—?"

Jake brought his hand out and laid it on top of hers. "No. My treat. I invited you."

He imagined a warm little current running from her hand to his. Maybe she felt it too, because her blue eyes looked at him uncertainly.

"Thank you." Her smile, so quick at the store, was a little dimmer out here.

"No problem." He returned her smile, hoping to bring up the wattage in hers. "I enjoyed the company."

That reserved look remained, and it dawned on him: this had started out as a friendly lunch, and he'd been all business. *Stupid.*

Jake set out his payment card in the plastic tray the waitress provided. He used his personal card rather than the corporate one, although the company paid for his meals when he was on the road. Mandy wouldn't be aware of the difference, but he'd know.

The waitress brought his card back, Jake signed the payment slip, and they rose to leave. "Mandy, I want to ask you two favors."

"What?"

"People don't know why I'm here yet. For the

first couple days, I'd like to keep it that way while I'm asking around about things. It's easier to get a natural answer when they're not thinking about why I'm asking. Could you not mention it to anyone yet?"

"Okay," she said cautiously.

"Number two." He drew himself up a little straighter and plunged ahead. "I just wasted a perfectly good lunch talking business with you. It's not what I planned on. Would you go out with me tonight? No shoptalk this time. I promise."

The faint furrows between her brows faded. "You mean, like dinner?"

"Dinner, maybe a movie—you name it."

She seemed . . . what? Unsure what he meant? Resistant to the idea? The sandwich he'd just eaten formed a ball in Jake's stomach. He must have come off like a real jerk.

"Okay," she said, still looking a little confounded.

"Where can I pick you up? I'll meet you at the store if that makes you more comfortable."

"Oh." She glanced down at her clothes. The simple blouse and slacks she wore now looked fine to Jake.

"You wouldn't need to change unless you really want to," he said. "That is, we could save the caviar and escargot for the second date. I mean, if you . . ." He trailed off.

And suddenly, there it was. A warm smile, worthy

of the ones he'd seen back at the store. Jake's stomach loosened.

"I was just thinking I should go home and get a sweater before we go. It gets a little chillier at night." Mandy dipped back down to the table and grabbed a paper napkin. "I'll write down directions."

"I have a GPS."

She fished a pen out of her purse. "The roads up here give GPS nightmares."

She leaned over the table, and Jake watched dark waves of hair fall against her cheek as she filled the napkin with a series of lines, curves, and captions with street names. To his relief, she added her address and phone number at the bottom. Which one would get him lost first, between Mandy's directions and his GPS—at this point, he couldn't tell.

He took the napkin from her and squinted. "Let's see. Turn left at the *X*, follow the squiggly line, make a right at the arrow—"

"Hush. You'll thank me."

They parted on the sidewalk, with Mandy heading back to her store while Jake continued his walking tour. He'd just had lunch, but he felt lighter as he headed down the street.

Then he rounded a corner, and his cell phone went crazy.

*Bzzt. Bzzt.*

He pulled the cumbersome thing out of his pocket and watched the messages load.

When it was over, he saw he'd missed eleven e-mails, three texts and a voice mail. Probably Mark at the home office, wondering if Jake had fallen into a hole. He scrolled back and found that the string of messages started at ten-fifteen. Obviously, Tall Pine was in a cell phone dead spot with occasional pockets of service.

Oddly enough, he hadn't even noticed until now.

Mandy-the-Christmas-girl had gotten him a little distracted.

He liked her. A lot. A light shroud of shyness seemed to surround her, but he hadn't seen a hint of it in the shop, or while she'd balked at the idea of his planting a hotel in her hometown. He wondered if she was right about the reaction he could expect from the rest of Tall Pine.

Jake thought about the look on her face when he told her why he'd come here. Startled. Disillusioned. Maybe even betrayed.

Almost like he'd told her there was no Santa Claus.

Mandy pushed open the door to The North Pole with enough speed to set the bells jangling instead of jingling. Mrs. Swanson's head jerked up from the stack of mail in her hands.

Mandy took a deep breath and slowed her pace.

**29**

She shouldn't come bursting in like a blizzard in the middle of August, even though that was exactly what she felt like. Her head was swirling with thoughts, and she couldn't seem to keep them going in any one direction.

"Hi," Mrs. Swanson said, and returned to the task of sifting through the envelopes.

She didn't say anything about Mandy's coming back half an hour late from lunch. Maybe she hadn't noticed. Mandy hadn't realized it herself until she was halfway down the block, when she suddenly remembered she had a watch and what it was for. She'd walked the rest of the way here double-time, and now she was trying to conceal the fact that she was out of breath. She drew in another deep breath as quietly as she could, and tried to act normally.

"Did I miss anything?" Mandy asked.

Mrs. Swanson looked up from the mail again to regard her quizzically.

Measuring her stride with care, Mandy walked behind the counter and stowed her purse. She had no idea what "normal" looked like at this point.

"Enjoy your lunch?"

"Sure. Chinese chicken salad. Can't go wrong there." Mandy smoothed at her hair. "The service was a little slow, though."

She should just own up to being late and apologize for it. But she wouldn't, for love or money, spill out the fact that she had a date tonight. With someone she'd just met. She was still processing it herself, and she wanted to see how it played out before she said anything about it.

The feather duster wasn't behind the counter where she'd left it, so Mrs. Swanson must have dusted, as she'd expected. What else would Mandy be doing, normally, right now?

"Mandy."

*Busted. She knows I was late. Okay, no big deal. . . .*

"You didn't even notice," Mrs. Swanson said. "You walked right past it."

Mandy followed the direction of her boss's nod and saw a large cardboard box alongside the counter. She would have had to make a much wider circle than usual to get behind the counter, and she hadn't even noticed. As she walked up to inspect it, she realized what had to be inside.

"The new keepsake ornaments!"

Okay, *that* was ridiculous. How could she have possibly missed seeing the package? Every year she looked forward to the latest line of Christmas ornaments, and they usually arrived by the end of July. The shipment had been delayed in transit, and it had been driving her nuts for two weeks.

*Head in the clouds much, Mandy?*

"I didn't think this was ever going to get here," Mandy stammered.

The box was still sealed. Because Mrs. Swanson knew that Mandy loved being the one to open it.

When she looked up, Mrs. Swanson had the

X-Acto knife in her hand. She passed it to Mandy with a flourish. Mandy grinned as she ceremoniously sliced open the box.

For the next hour, she no longer had to worry about what she would normally do. Taking out the new ornaments and setting up the display was a labor of love. This time of year, they would occupy the wall on the south side of the store. By November, they'd be front and center. Mandy lifted each one out with relish. Charlie Brown characters, Barbie and Winnie-the-Pooh were always staples, and she enjoyed seeing them. But her favorites were the trees, the snowmen, the reindeer . . . new versions of the old favorites.

They never could get Santa Claus quite the way she remembered him, though. She supposed her memory could be faulty, but she'd never met anyone to compare notes with. At least, she'd never met an adult who admitted to seeing him.

As she started to hang this year's Santa ornament on the display, she let it dangle from her fingers for a moment. Merry eyes, rosy cheeks, laughing face—a lot of detail had gone into the tiny figure, and it was well done. What was missing?

Her mind went back to her low-lit living room— that face, solemn and friendly at the same time. He'd looked right *at* her, and that memory still brought a flush of warmth whenever she thought about it. The memory had sustained her through all the kidding over the years, reminding her that there was goodness in the world, withstanding all the moments of doubt and discouragement.

Who in the world could capture that in a two-inch ornament?

Mandy smiled to herself as she hung the well-intended decoration in its place on the display. Then her eyes went to the framed clippings on the wall a few feet away.

Jake hadn't made it over to this side of the store. If he had, she wondered what he would have thought.

She wondered if she'd still have the same plans for the evening.

Just about everyone in town knew her story. Anyone who might have forgotten had a solid reminder, in those clippings and in Mandy's very presence in this store.

*You could have worked at a clothing store. You could have waited tables. Maybe even gone into real estate. Or moved somewhere else.*

Instead, she'd chosen to embrace her encounter with Santa as a blessing, not a curse. She'd stayed in Tall Pine, in the same house where she and her mother had lived before Mom passed away three years ago. Maybe, if Mandy had grown up in a big city instead of a small town, as time went on no one would have given her belief a second thought. But somehow, in Tall Pine, it had become part of her identity. When Mandy did go out on dates—both in high school and afterward—the conversation always worked its way around to: *"Do you still believe . . ."*

And Jake didn't know about any of it.

The idea was freeing. No history of past embarrassing moments, no debate over whether she still believed what she'd seen. A clean slate.

She hung a gingerbread man on the display hook designated for him, then stepped back to survey her work.

Mrs. Swanson came to stand alongside her. "It looks good."

An unusual comment from her boss, especially on a predesigned display.

Mandy should never underestimate her. Of course she'd noticed Mandy was late coming back from lunch, and her attempts to pass for normal apparently weren't making the grade.

She kept trying anyway. "I think the snowman's my favorite. The eyes really do look like coal, and the carrot nose is perfect."

Mrs. Swanson fingered the snowman's tiny woolen scarf with a nod.

To Mandy's gratitude, more customers found their way into the store over the course of the afternoon. It kept her busy and helped the time go a little faster. She kept watching the clock, which wasn't hard to do; clocks were everywhere, in the shapes of wreaths, stars and pinecones.

Usually Mrs. Swanson left around four, about an hour before the store closed. *Watch today be the exception,* Mandy thought. But at ten after four, Mrs. Swanson gathered up her purse and headed for the exit.

"Good night." The older woman opened the door to the sunny mid-August sidewalk. "If you can call it that."

It wouldn't be dark until after eight. "Good night," Mandy said.

For the next half hour, Mandy fussed and tidied, waiting on one customer who sighed over the keepsake ornaments, but didn't buy anything.

Twenty minutes to five. Outside, the foot traffic didn't lessen, although the passersby walked more briskly, probably on their way to find a spot for an early dinner. Mandy watched and waited until she didn't see anyone near the door. Then she walked over to the framed clippings.

She picked up the recent one, the one with the very recognizable photo of herself standing behind the counter. It was in a simple document frame, nothing too expensive. Taking another look toward the door, Mandy set the clipping on the edge of a nearby display table. Then she nudged it, bit by bit, until it dropped to the floor with a small sound of breaking glass.

Now she could tell Mrs. Swanson, truthfully, that it fell.

# Chapter 3

Jake navigated the road slowly, keeping a vigilant eye out for the final turn. Mandy's directions had taken him down a series of streets that weren't clearly marked; he never should have laughed at the landmarks she'd supplied. His GPS had proven useless because, as soon as he turned off Evergreen Lane, his phone lost the signal. He should have seen that one coming, as sporadic as his reception had been all day.

He was pretty sure he'd found the right house even before the number on the mailbox confirmed it. Bright red geraniums spilled out of a window box, and a painted birdhouse—red and green, natch—hung on the porch that ran in front of the little wooden home. The exterior was fashioned like a log cabin, and the varnished wood had been allowed to keep its natural color rather than being painted over.

Jake pulled up the steep driveway, climbed a

narrow wooden stairway to her front door and rang the bell.

Moments later, Mandy opened the door wearing a royal blue blouse that brought out the color of her eyes. She seemed slightly taller than she had this afternoon; Jake looked down to see the pointed toes of black dress shoes poking out from beneath her black slacks. She'd traded in the silver bell earrings for little gold hoops, and she carried a sweater over her arm. Her purse was already on her shoulder.

"Hey," she said with a shy smile, slipping out the door so quickly she might have been hiding a body inside. Then again, Jake wouldn't be anxious for anyone else to see his apartment if he hadn't been expecting company ahead of time.

"Hey." Maybe it was their snappy repartee, but Jake flashed back to those early dates he'd had in high school. He felt a trace of that awkward, new-shoe feeling. Not quite what he expected at the age of twenty-nine. Awkward, but kind of exciting, too. Walking beside her, Jake caught a light scent that reminded him a little of cinnamon and a little of the shop where she worked, with some sweet, indefinable tang that wasn't quite like anything he could think of.

When they reached his rented pickup truck in the driveway, Jake explained, "The limo was in the shop."

She looked at him, puzzled. He opened the door for her and gave her a hand up. "I rented it for the four-wheel drive," he explained. "I figured I might be checking out some undeveloped land up here while I'm looking for a location for the hotel. Plus," he admitted, "it's just fun to drive it."

He rounded the truck to the other side and climbed into the driver's seat. Mandy was still quiet. He remembered something else about those high school days: wishing he could cut straight to that first kiss to get it out of the way. Partly to get rid of the suspense, knowing the moment was hours away. Partly because he just plain wanted to kiss her.

Something about the way she was perched on the passenger seat told Jake she was every bit as nervous as he was, probably more so. He thought a quick kiss would put him at ease. He also thought it would make Mandy Reese jump out of her skin.

He ventured a hand on her wrist, and she actually did jump a little. But it got her to look at him, rather than at some undetermined spot on the dashboard.

He smiled at her and got one back. "Where to? I'm the new guy in town. I'm at your mercy."

Her words spilled out quickly. "There's a steak place a couple of blocks past Evergreen Lane that's pretty good. It's not super fancy."

He wondered if she was worrying about his joke about caviar and escargot.

"Steak it is." He started the car. This time of summer, six p.m. was still broad daylight. It felt a little early for dinner. "Would you like to walk around town a little first?"

She hesitated. "You know, I'd better not. I twisted my ankle this afternoon. I was standing on a stepladder, and . . . I sort of stepped wrong when I got down. It's not bad. But I probably shouldn't do much walking tonight."

Jake didn't comment as he backed down the driveway. But something about her answer didn't quite ring true.

Especially coming from a woman who was wearing high heels tonight, when she hadn't been this afternoon.

Mandy had only been to Barrymore's Steakhouse once before, on an ill-fated date a couple of years ago. Fact: still believing in Santa Claus at the age of twenty-two made even the former high school chess-club champion feel cool by comparison. He'd laughed at her. Then tried to backtrack. The evening had never quite recovered, and she hadn't gone out with him again.

She wasn't going to let that happen tonight.

If Jake stayed around very long, it was just a

matter of time before he heard she'd seen Santa Claus. But like Cinderella with her conjured dress and pumpkin coach, Mandy wanted at least one night of being normal. Of not trying to explain herself.

"That'll be all. Thanks." Jake handed the menus back to the waiter, a thirtyish blond man she didn't recognize. It was the main reason she'd chosen this restaurant. At any of the places on Evergreen Lane, someone on the staff was likely to be an old classmate, or one of their siblings. It was a wonder that Mandy hadn't known the girl who took their order at the Pine 'n' Dine this afternoon.

"So, I promised you no shoptalk," Jake said. "Tonight it's your turn. Has Christmas always been a big deal for you?"

"Always." *If you only knew.* "I know some people get tired of it. I've just never been one of them."

"Oh, I think most people like Christmas. It's just that for most people, once a year is enough."

"You know, people say that to me all the time. But they still come into the store." A smile touched her lips. "You did."

"You've got me there."

Jake had changed into a crisp white shirt with a deep brown tie and a tweedy light brown jacket. Almost like the kind of coat professors were supposed to wear, except that he looked way too young to be a professor. He managed to look dressy and casual at the same time. She knew he'd never been here before, but there was something in the way he sat back from the table that gave the impression of comfort.

Mandy picked up her water glass. "Here's what I see every day. Some customers are like me. They love it right away. Then there are the ones like you. Their first reaction is, 'What the heck?' But they come in a little farther, like they're trying to figure it out. They look around, they hear the music . . . and it usually happens. They get that Christmas feeling."

Jake's eyes glinted. "And they usually buy something."

"Well, usually. But that's not the point."

"Sure it is. The store's in business to make money."

"Okay. But what do the customers get out of it?" When he didn't reply, she answered for him: "A little piece of Christmas."

"You're right. If a business doesn't supply a benefit, it doesn't stay in business. But for you, that little piece of Christmas is there twelve months a year. Doesn't it get . . ."

"Less special? Not for me." Mandy considered. "The way I see it, those other eleven months out of the year—they're mine. When the whole world isn't surrounded by Christmas, and people aren't so busy getting stressed out about it, they come into

The North Pole and just *enjoy* it. And I get to give them that."

Jake nodded. He seemed satisfied. Maybe even impressed. "You win." He picked up his glass of soda. "I'm not a total Scrooge, by the way."

"Not many people are. It's just easy to lose sight of Christmas when you're right in the middle of it. What's Christmas like for you?"

"Well, it's the one day of the year I know I won't be working."

Mandy flinched. "Seriously?"

"Okay, I'm exaggerating. It's a couple of days. And I always spend it with my family. It's . . ." He shook his head with a smile. "Chaos. Complete and utter chaos. My dad calls it the annual invasion."

That sounded better. "Relatives?"

He nodded. "Two days before Christmas, everyone converges on my parents' house. And I mean *everyone*. There's me, my mom and dad, my older brother and his wife. They have a little girl, Emily. That's who the pinecone necklace is for. But then there are aunts, uncles, cousins . . . and tons of food. My mom cooks a lot of it, but everyone brings more. There are kids you haven't seen for a year, so you're trying to keep everybody's name straight, what grade they're in, and who got their braces off, and it doesn't really matter because you can't hear a thing."

"It sounds wonderful."

"I guess it is." His gaze drifted past her, and Mandy knew he wasn't seeing the inside of the restaurant at all. "The only one who's not making a racket is my dad. He'll sit in his armchair while everybody's rushing around. He acts like he thinks everybody else is nuts, but you can tell he loves it. But by the next day, everybody clears out to go to their own homes. My brother and his family usually stay a little later. It's amazing how much quieter the house seems with only six people in it."

"And Christmas Eve?"

"Really quiet. Lots of last-minute preparations behind closed doors. Then usually we'll watch a movie. It's kind of the calm after the chaos. Then in the morning, we open presents and go out to breakfast. But the best part is all the buildup."

Mandy nodded. "That's because when it comes, it's over so fast."

"Unless you work at a Christmas store."

"It helps."

Jake picked up his drink. "What about you? What do you do for Christmas?"

"A little quieter than that. The last couple of years, I've had dinner at Mrs. Swanson's. She's the owner of the shop. This year I think I'm going to invite her over instead. I've never cooked a turkey by myself before."

He frowned. "Where's your family?"

Mandy took in a deep, slow breath. "I lost my

mom three years ago. Everybody else is out of state."

Jake looked startled. He set down his glass. "She couldn't have been very old. What happened?"

"An aneurysm. One of those things you don't see coming. She was forty-seven."

"What about your father?"

"They got divorced when I was eight." She felt a tight smile cross her face. "He came to the funeral."

"I'm sorry. I had no idea."

"Of course you didn't. You just met me." She shook her head. "But it's okay. The thing about my mom . . ." She stirred her iced tea with her straw, aware of Jake's eyes on her. "She did so much, and I just didn't realize it. You don't think about those things when you're a kid. She must have worked so hard. She worked at the bank up here, so I was a latchkey kid, but when she got home, she always had time for me. She made sure I knew I was important to her. We never had a lot of extra, but we didn't need much."

She didn't go into the rest of it. After her mother died, Mandy found out just how hard her mother had worked to make sure her daughter would be all right. The house was paid off, so it was Mandy's, free and clear. There had even been an insurance policy for good measure. Not bad for a reluctantly single mother.

Mandy tried to put her finger on what she wanted to say. "I wish I could have had her longer. Of course. But . . . she left me with something. She made me want to make other people happy. Maybe that's what my job is really about."

Jake studied her, his eyes quiet and direct. She just hoped he didn't feel sorry for her.

"I've never met anyone like you," he said finally.

By the time they left the restaurant, the sky was darkening, and a chill had crept into the air. Mandy slipped her sweater on. As they walked toward the car's parking spot alongside the curb, Jake took her hand. Her fingers curled around his, and she was surprised how comfortable it felt.

"Still up for a movie?" he asked.

She hesitated for an instant. "Sure."

Tall Pine Cineplex was the only theater in town. On a Saturday night, there was an awfully good chance she might run into someone from her old school there, and there was no telling where the conversation might go. She'd just have to think on her feet.

Jake stopped and turned her toward him just before they reached the car. "Mandy."

She hadn't realized until now just how much taller he was; even in her heels, she needed to tilt her head back to look up at him.

His eyes were fixed on hers in that direct stare she was beginning to know. Now he seemed as

**45**

close to being uncertain as she'd seen tonight. Somehow, Mandy found that reassuring.

"There's something I've been wanting to do for a while," he said. "And I'm hoping you won't mind."

He stepped down from the curb, taking his height down several inches. He still stood taller than Mandy, but now his mouth was just slightly above hers. Jake lifted his hand and ran a finger lightly down the side of her cheek. There was no mistaking what he meant.

Mandy thought of the way it felt when she jumped into the cold water of the Tall Pine pond on a hot summer day. *I'm not ready for this. . . .*

Running his fingers underneath her jawline, Jake tipped her chin up toward him. Her heart was thrumming so loudly she was sure he could hear it.

*I haven't had nearly enough practice at this. . . .*

His lips met hers lightly, and Mandy felt something inside melt. She closed her eyes and drank in the warmth, the softness, the nearness. His other hand came up to frame her face. The kiss was gentle, unhurried, and the street around them felt unusually still. It was as if the world had paused.

*Oh, I could do a lot more of this.*

Her knees were shaking, so she brought her arms up around his waist and held on.

Why had she thought she needed a sweater?

After another long, melting moment, he lifted

his head and smiled. "I hope you don't mind," he repeated.

Mandy didn't trust her voice. She nodded. Then shook her head.

She felt light as a feather, and she knew it was too good to be true. She might not turn into a pumpkin at midnight, but this couldn't last. A little voice in her head nagged her: *You know you can't keep this up, right?*

She brushed the little voice aside with, *I can try.*

"Okay," Jake said as they edged forward in line outside the movie theater. "The truth."

Mandy, who seemed vaguely distracted, turned with a start. "What?"

He nodded at the list of films on the marquee above. "Which ones have you seen already?"

She bit her lip, an innocent gesture that reminded him of their kiss with a pleasant rush that nearly derailed his train of thought. "None of them, actually."

If you eliminated the movies Jake had already seen, that took them down to two out of six. But that wasn't a problem. On the other hand . . . "Not a big movie fan?"

The line inched forward. "No, I just—don't go out much. But I watch a lot of movies at home."

A sweet, pretty girl like her? Then again, maybe

it wasn't a complete surprise. There was something sheltered about her, a sense of innocence he couldn't quite define.

He turned his attention back to the marquee. The two lines were fairly long—obviously, Tall Pine Cineplex did good business on a Saturday night—so that bought them a little time. "Well, I can vouch for the thriller," he said. "The romantic comedy, not so much."

She frowned. "If you've already seen—"

"Not an issue. A good movie is worth seeing more than once. Even a half-decent movie."

They settled on the tearjerker drama—one of the two movies, as it turned out, that Jake hadn't seen.

"Okay, your turn," Mandy said. "The truth. What's your most re-watched movie of all time?"

He squirmed. "Remember, I'm an addict. My tastes go pretty far back."

She tilted her head expectantly. He sighed.

"If I'm in the mood for a no-brainer, the original *Planet of the Apes*. If I'm in the mood for quality—*Casablanca.*"

She responded immediately. "I love *Casablanca.*"

He stared at her. "Most people I know are allergic to black-and-white."

"It was my mom's favorite."

Jake stepped forward to fill the gap that had opened in front of them as they continued to compare notes. Most of Mandy's favorites were more recent, but he agreed with a lot of her choices: *A Beautiful Mind, Cast Away, Erin Brockovich.*

"You lose me on the musicals, though," he said. "I know it's poetic license, but I can't get past the idea of characters bursting into song in the middle of . . ."

He'd lost her. She was studying the wall on their right, as if the posters of coming attractions were suddenly of intense interest. Jake had to nudge her when it was time to edge up in line again. When she moved forward, she kept her head turned toward the wall of posters.

"Earth to Mandy," he said when it was their turn at the ticket window.

She blushed as they stepped forward, and Jake saw her eyes flicker toward the line of people at their left.

*Furtive* and Mandy didn't go hand-in-hand, or at least he wouldn't have thought so. As Jake ordered the tickets, his eyes followed the direction where Mandy's had flickered. He didn't see anything unusual—but then, he didn't know any of the people in the line alongside them.

He suspected Mandy did.

His first, territorial instinct said *ex-boyfriend.* But as the girl at the window slid their tickets forward, his glance didn't turn up any likely candidates. An elderly couple, a middle-aged woman, two women about Mandy's age . . .

Jake marveled at the way Mandy kept him between herself and the people they walked past, using him as a human shield. She didn't relax until they were halfway down the corridor that led to their theater.

"See somebody you hate?" he asked.

"What?" She gave him a startled look, but her face was still flushed. Not a bad actress, but not a great one either.

"Whoever you saw back there."

"Oh. No, just . . . it's awkward."

She didn't elaborate. And as they made their way down the slightly slanted floor in search of seats, Jake observed that she didn't appear to be limping at all in her heels.

He decided to leave it alone for now. There could be all kinds of explanations. It could be an old hurt or a recent argument. Or, in a small town like this, maybe she didn't want to arouse a lot of curiosity on a first date.

Then again, maybe Jake wouldn't like the answer. Maybe she just didn't want to be seen with the troublemaker from the big city.

But later that night, when he took her home and kissed her at the top of the stairs leading to her front door, none of that mattered. He'd wondered if kissing her earlier in the evening might make the good-night kiss anticlimactic. It didn't.

*Take it slow,* a voice in his head said. *Just because it feels right . . .*

He'd learned his lesson long ago—he hoped—about relationships built on physical attraction. Not every difference could be dissolved with a kiss.

But for tonight, it was good enough.

Mandy closed the front door behind her and allowed herself the luxury of leaning against it for a moment with her eyes closed.

Things like this didn't happen in her world. She didn't go out with men she didn't know. In fact, she hardly ever *met* men she didn't know, unless you counted the ones who came into the shop with their wives.

It couldn't last. She was Mandy Claus. Spotting Julie Ashman at the theater tonight had been a reminder of that.

But, with her feet barely touching the floor of her living room, Mandy wanted to keep things just like this for as long as she could. That meant dealing with certain realities.

Knowing what she was facing, she opened her eyes.

She'd let it go too far, and she'd known it for some time. It looked too much like The North Pole.

A Christmas wreath still hung over the fireplace mantel, which was decorated with half a dozen nutcracker figurines, a swag of green garland hanging below. There were Christmas candleholders on most of the shelves, snow globes, snowmen . . . everything but a Christmas tree. That, she didn't have, because she always brought home a fresh one.

In the three years since her mom died, it had gotten harder and harder to put Christmas away when it was over. So, every year, more of the decorations had stayed out. This year Mandy hadn't even tried to box any of it up. She didn't want to pack away all the good memories, all the warmth they represented. She'd clutched Christmas around her like a security blanket, and it hadn't seemed to matter because she didn't really have guests here. And it was impossible to resist bringing new things home from the shop.

Mom had been the voice of reason: *"If we left the Christmas things out all year round, it wouldn't be as special."* They'd always left a few decorations out as a reminder—that cardinal snow globe, for instance—but most of the house had returned to normal the first week in January.

Mandy closed her eyes again, listening to her mother's voice in her mind. The thought of packing Christmas up made her throat feel tight, but she'd managed it until these past few years. It was what the rest of the world did. Then, she reminded herself, they had the fun of taking it out again every year after Thanksgiving.

She could do this. And if Mom could see her, she'd be proud.

Mandy opened her eyes once more and gulped. It could wait until tomorrow. But tomorrow, she had her work cut out for her.

# Chapter 4

"It fell," Mandy explained Monday morning.

Mrs. Swanson studied her dubiously, then looked again at the wall where the framed newspaper clippings had hung.

"The glass cracked," Mandy added. "I'll pick up a new frame the next chance I get."

"What about the other clipping?"

Mandy followed Mrs. Swanson's eyes to the wall, where a couple of snowman prints now hung from the nails that had held the clippings.

"One clipping looked funny without the other one. It was . . . out of balance."

Mrs. Swanson was silent.

"It's still August," Mandy went on. "I didn't think it would matter too much."

If she'd been hooked up to a lie detector, she was sure the thing would have smoke coming out of it by now.

"Well, get it back up there as soon as you can," Mrs. Swanson said.

Mrs. Swanson crossed the store and turned around the OPEN sign. Mandy had painted the hanging wooden plaque herself five years ago, decorating it with candy canes at the corners and strands of holly garland around the edges.

"So," Mrs. Swanson said, "what did you do this weekend?"

Had she ever asked Mandy that question before? Mandy couldn't remember. Then again, most weekends, the answer wouldn't have been so memorable.

"Went to the movies." *With a date.* Mandy knew for a fact she'd never told Mrs. Swanson about her one evening with the chess-club champ. To cut off a possible follow-up question, Mandy continued, "And started a housecleaning project. It was way overdue. I accumulate too much stuff."

"It's easy to do."

Mandy grinned. "Especially when you work in a place like this."

She thought of Mrs. Swanson's home. She'd only seen it when it was decorated for Christmas, but even then, it was tidy and precise . . . and probably a little less yuletide-heavy than Mandy's house had been up until yesterday. She'd left the living room at a disastrous halfway point, with most of the Christmas items boxed up, but without having tackled the problem of fitting them into the hall closet. There was space in her mother's bedroom, but she didn't want to do that. She'd never decided what to do with that room, but turning it into a storage area would be awful.

"What did *you* do this weekend?" Mandy asked. Okay, they had had this conversation a few times.

"Well, I saw a movie too," Mrs. Swanson said. "But mine was on television."

"I don't suppose it was *Ghost*." Mandy had been trying to get Mrs. Swanson to watch it for years.

"No, I told you, I think those things are silly."

"You know what we're going to do this year?" Mandy said. "I'm going to cook Christmas dinner at my house. And before you leave I'll *make* you watch it."

Mrs. Swanson pursed her lips. "We'll see."

Mandy wondered if Jake would like it or not. Their discussion hadn't gotten around to much fantasy, although he'd confessed a fondness for the old monster movies from the thirties and forties. The Frankenstein monster, he maintained, was a nice guy. Just really misunderstood.

Movies. Jake.

And just like that, an idea blossomed in her head.

Mandy got busy rotating the stock of greeting cards, trying to keep her mind occupied, but the idea kept growing, and the more she thought about it, the better it sounded.

She waited for her break to call him, so she wouldn't use Mrs. Swanson's time. She used her cell phone, so she could make the call outside.

Jake's phone rang. One thing about Mount Douglas compared to Tall Pine: the cell reception was much more consistent. He stepped out of the path of a passing couple to answer it.

"Jake Wyndham."

"Jake? It's Mandy."

There was no denying, or fighting, the lift he felt at the sound of her voice. He tried not to grin like a sap in the middle of the sidewalk. "What's up?"

"I've got an idea."

He waited for her to go on. She didn't. "That sounds mysterious."

"I think it'd be better if I took you to see it. Is there any chance you could come by the store a little after five?"

*They shouldn't close so early,* his mental accountant interjected. "Sure."

"Your four-wheel-drive might come in handy." He was pretty sure he heard a smile in her voice, too.

More mystery. "Okay, you're on. I'll see you five-ish."

Jake disconnected the call and glanced around

at the main street of Mount Douglas—named, imaginatively enough, Main Street. He felt absurdly guilty, as if he'd been cheating on Mandy. Or on Tall Pine.

After her warnings about the problems he might run into with the town officials, he'd decided this morning to look into a Plan B for the hotel location. His boss didn't know he was here, and Jake thought he might keep it that way. Nearly an hour farther up in the mountains than Tall Pine, Mount Douglas was substantially larger. It had a ski resort, multiple hotels and numerous fast-food franchise restaurants. He only saw two national chain hotels, but that told him if they decided to open a Regal Hotel up here, they probably wouldn't get any argument from the city.

It also felt less like a picturesque mountain town, and more like Anywhere, U.S.A.

It'd be an easier undertaking. And it would make less of a difference. Whether they liked it or not, the fact was, a town like Tall Pine could use the additional business a place like a Regal Hotel could bring in.

Jake checked the time on his phone. Twelve-thirty. Plenty of time to do some exploring here, just for the sake of argument, and still get back to Mandy's store by five o'clock.

Instead, he went back to the truck and drove

through McDonald's—it might be the last one of those he'd see in a while—then headed back to Tall Pine.

Mandy watched the businesses thin as the pickup traveled down the main highway through the far end of Tall Pine. She saw Jake watching the road ahead, from time to time casting a curious glance at her.

As dry, grassy fields started to appear between the businesses, Jake quirked a smile at her. "This must be a field trip in the literal sense."

"We're almost there." Mandy spotted the road sign up ahead. "Make a quick right up here."

Jake turned.

Seconds later, Mandy spotted it. "Over here on the right."

Jake's eyes followed, and she watched recognition dawn. He stopped the truck. "Would you look at that."

His expression was everything she'd hoped for, maybe more. A kid's expression of discovery and near awe.

About five hundred yards across the field, facing away from the main highway, was a worn old drive-in movie screen, half-concealed by trees and brush.

"We can get closer if you want," she said. "That's

why I thought of the four-wheel drive. It's pretty overgrown."

With a grin, Jake turned right and drove toward the screen, the truck taking a bumpy series of small hills and dips as it went.

"The rises are still here," he said. "You'd park your car on sort of a hill, and the older drive-ins had posts for these tinny-sounding speakers you'd hang on your car window."

Even in the pickup, which sat higher than the average car, Mandy could feel the tall brush scraping the bottom of the vehicle. Several hundred feet from the screen, they reached the last of the rises. The ground in front of it scooped a little lower, and the dry grass between the truck and the screen grew lower, more level.

Jake came to a stop, facing the weather-beaten screen head-on. "Front-row seats."

"It's less than ten minutes from Evergreen Lane," she said. "There's a ton of space, it's right off the road, and it's sat for so long, I think your company might be able to get a really good deal on it."

She wasn't sure if Jake heard her. His eyes were still devouring the sight before him as if it were the ruins of an ancient civilization. "This is awesome," he said. "Want to get out?"

"Sure."

As Jake climbed out, Mandy started to open her

own door, then remembered to wait while he rounded the front of the truck to open it for her. He was nice about those things, and she enjoyed it.

He took her hand to help her down, and she landed on both feet, knee-deep in brush.

He kept her hand. "Is your ankle okay?" His eyes were fixed on her face.

She felt herself flush.

"It's fine," she said. "It was a false alarm."

He held her gaze long enough to tell her he didn't buy it, knew she'd made it up. She wasn't any good at this lying business. Mandy could imagine what it would be like to be someone opposing Jake at a business meeting. He didn't seem likely to be the first to back down. That might help him when it came to the town council. It sure wasn't helping Mandy right now.

He turned back toward the screen. "How long has it been vacant? Did you ever go to the movies here?"

"Once or twice. It would've been almost twenty years ago. I came here with my parents when I was little." She would have had to be really little, if her dad had still been around. "My father left when I was eight, so I was maybe six or seven. I don't remember when it closed down."

Jake's fingers curled slightly around hers, and Mandy felt a reaction she would never have expected: a lump in her throat. Her father had left her. That was old news, a fact of life, not something she gave much thought.

"What movie did you see?"

She wasn't ready for the softness in his voice, either. But she didn't want him feeling sorry for her. She let his hand go and stepped toward the screen, trying to picture the details in her mind. "I can't remember. It wasn't a cartoon, and it didn't have animals in it, so I must have been pretty bored. I know I fell asleep." She thought about the dark backseat and remembered: "They had me wear my pajamas. We even brought my pillow along."

He stepped past her, examining the screen. "I didn't go to my first drive-in till I was nineteen. They still have a few of them in Pennsylvania, but nothing too close to where I lived. We drove over an hour to get there, and my girlfriend thought I was nuts. She didn't get it at all." He turned toward her with a grin. "It really was a lousy way to see a movie. The sound's terrible, the picture's dim . . . but it's all about the experience."

"A dark, lo-fi movie?"

"It's—nostalgic. Americana. You see the movie in your car, and it's your own private environment. Families could bring their kids in their pajamas and not worry if they were too noisy for the people in the next row. And drive-ins were huge with teenagers. Lots of making out in the backseat.

People used to call them 'passion pits.' Kids didn't always see the movie."

Mandy couldn't resist. "So, what about you? Did you watch the movie?"

"I was nineteen."

"Still a teenager."

"Barely. And remember, I went there as a film connoisseur." One corner of his mouth twitched up. "Plus, like I said, my girlfriend was annoyed." Taking longer strides through the brittle weeds, Jake picked his way across the now-imaginary front row. "Any idea of the lot size? Or who owns it?"

"No."

A late afternoon wind blew thick brown hair into Jake's eyes. He shook it back. "It's a little far from town. . . ."

"But not too far." Mandy had tried to anticipate the drawbacks. "Your hotel has the name recognition factor, and people could find it online. The local hotels would still have a shot at customers, too, and the town council would like that."

"Cooperative competition. Set it up as a win-win." Jake squinted thoughtfully and nodded. "It might fly."

"I hoped you'd like it."

"It'd need a lot of work. The land would have to be leveled. . . ." He shook his head. "Isn't this dumb? I almost hate to mess with it. It's like an archaeological site or something." He flattened a section of brush with his shoe and peered down. "Is that what I think it is?"

He knelt to brush aside more of the dead grass. Mandy hurried over. "Watch out for snakes."

"Now you tell—look at this!"

She bent to see what he'd found. Based on Jake's reaction, it could have been a million dollars, or at least a gold brick.

Barely visible through the weeds, still half-buried in the dirt, a rusted metal speaker poked up from the ground.

"They never got around to renovating this theater," Jake said. "That's the coolest thing ever." He looked up at her with a self-conscious grin. "Okay, maybe not *ever*. But still. Later on drive-ins had these wires that clipped to your car antenna, or they just broadcast the sound at a low frequency, so you listened through your car radio. Lots of dead batteries by the end of the show."

Jake brushed at the dirt again, then straightened. "However. It's good and buried in there. An excavation project for another day. And I should probably get you away from here before we find one of your snakes."

This time he took her by the elbow, rather than her hand, as they walked back to the truck and got inside. After Jake climbed up beside her, he started to put the keys in the ignition, then stopped and turned to her.

"Thanks for this. It was really nice of you to bring me here. I'll need to look at some other spots, too, but this has definite possibilities." He smiled. "Although part of me kind of wishes I could turn it back into what it used to be."

"It'd be fun. At least, until you went broke."

"Which is where the business part of my brain kicks in." His smile faded, and his eyes grew serious. "You see—the business side isn't such a bad thing. It's what pays the bills."

Mandy nodded. "I know. But I'm not the one you need to convince."

"Right." He put the keys in the ignition, but once again, he didn't start the car. Instead, he turned to face her, as much as the front seat of the truck would allow. "Mandy, there's something I want to get out of the way."

She waited.

"I'm going to start asking around about available property in the next couple of days. This spot, for one. When I do that, people are going to know why I came to Tall Pine pretty quick."

She tried to anticipate his train of thought. "So, you want me to wait until that happens, and after that, I won't need to worry about mentioning it to other people."

"Right. But there's something else you need to worry about, and I think you know what that is."

He fixed her with the same direct stare she'd seen earlier, when he asked about her ankle.

Mandy felt a tickle of apprehension.

He rested his left hand on top of the steering wheel. "You might not want to be seen with the guy from the big-city hotel chain. From what you've told me, there's probably going to be some friction about that. Whatever kind of flack you might get . . . you probably know more about what to expect than I do. But maybe you don't want to deal with it."

He seemed to be waiting for her response. Mandy wasn't sure where he was going with this, so she had no idea what to say.

"I'd like to keep seeing you," Jake said. "But I get the impression you haven't been anxious to be seen with me in public, and I don't want to feel like we're supposed to hide. In a town this size, maybe that'd make things too awkward for you. I can understand that. But I don't want to be a deep, dark secret. If you're not okay with that, just tell me now and I'll get out of your hair. No hard feelings. Seriously."

Those brown eyes looked at her steadily. It took several seconds for his meaning to sink in.

*That's* why he thought she'd fibbed about a hurt ankle, and ducked her old classmate at the movie theater.

"Jake, I—" She started to correct him and stopped.

Maybe the easiest thing was just to let him think that. The truth was a lot more complicated.

He kept his eyes on hers, his expression almost unnervingly calm. Mandy shifted her gaze back to his hand, resting on top of the steering wheel.

Not just resting on it. Gripping it.

As if what she said next really mattered to him.

She took a deep breath and picked her next words carefully. "I didn't mean to act like there was anything wrong with being seen with you."

"But? Is there a disclaimer coming?" He could certainly put things in businesslike terms.

"No buts. I'd love to keep going out with you. In public." She'd just have to take her chances.

His eyes lost some of their serious look, and Mandy saw his hand on the wheel relax perceptibly. Her heart kicked up.

"You're sure?" Jake smiled. "People aren't going to throw rocks at you?"

"Well, not for *that.*"

Mandy tried to keep her thoughts clear. He'd been open and direct with her; he'd stuck his neck out. She could do the same. Instead of taking the safe route, she could repay honesty with honesty. She should do it. This was a perfect time.

She tried to imagine telling him: *Jake, I believe in Santa Claus.*

Instantly, she pictured the look on his face: disbelief, maybe followed by amusement. Or a hint of pity. She'd seen those expressions too many times growing up. She didn't want to see any of them on Jake. Not now. Not unless there was no way around it.

He saw her for what she was—most of it, anyway—without the preconceptions of everyone else in town. He liked what he saw. And she liked the way he looked at her.

*Let me have this. At least for a while.*

It was August. Things were quieter at the store. His hotel project might not even get off the ground, and he could be gone before the Christmas season even started. She didn't like to think that way, but it was a possibility.

Maybe he'd never know.

And maybe the Brooklyn Bridge was still for sale.

Jake pulled her out of her thoughts. "You've got another reason to worry about your reputation, you know."

She eyed him cautiously. "What do you mean?"

"Well, here we are at the drive-in. I told you, everyone knows what goes on at these places."

His grin was teasing, and once again, Mandy felt light as a feather. A feeling that she was just where she belonged, because she knew exactly what to say.

**68**

"I feel pretty safe," she said. "After all, this truck doesn't have a backseat."

His eyes glimmered as if she'd challenged him with a dare. Before she knew it, he'd pulled her into another delicious kiss. It was several minutes before either of them spoke again.

When Jake lifted his lips from hers, he tucked a strand of hair behind her ear. "So, can I take you out to dinner again tonight? In front of God and everybody?"

Not trusting her voice, Mandy nodded.

# Chapter 5

Jake stepped out of Tall Pine's only commercial real estate agency with five property listings and a promise from the real estate agent to track down the out-of-town owner of the old drive-in site.

Inside, he'd gotten his first taste of what Mandy had warned him about. When he went in asking about property, the receptionist's eyebrows had shot up. He felt like the guy in the movies who strolled into the saloon saying he was looking for the fastest gun in the West.

He fired up the truck and went to check out the other properties. The agent had offered to take him out to look, but he hadn't seemed too disappointed when Jake said he wanted to do the initial exploring on his own. No high pressure there, but then, the man might not have taken him seriously. Jake had probably looked like a kid with a checkbook, possibly an empty one at that. It wouldn't be the first time he'd been taken for a guy fresh out of college. Sometimes there were advantages to being underestimated.

Once he brought up Regal Hotels, it would be a different ball game.

He checked out the locations and made conscientious notes of the pros and cons. By lunchtime, he gave in to the magnetic pull of The North Pole. After all, he had to eat, and there was no reason he had to do it alone.

But when he walked into the store, he didn't see Mandy. Instead, a woman with glasses and meticulous dark gray hair stood behind the counter. Mrs. Swanson, at a guess.

He considered feigning some browser-type behavior while he waited to see if Mandy emerged from the stock room, but decided to stick with the direct approach. As he walked up to the counter, Jake found himself standing a little straighter. For some reason he'd pictured Mrs. Swanson as a grandmotherly, Mrs. Santa Claus type. Based on her professional demeanor, that wasn't the case. "Is Mandy here?"

"She's off today." The steel-haired woman inclined her head slightly. "Are you the gentleman from Hallmark?"

"No, I'm Jake Wyndham." His name didn't appear to ring any bells. "It's not business."

He wondered if any vendors' reps came around the store to see Mandy on not-business.

Maybe not, because the woman's eyebrows lifted

a fraction. As her glance passed over him again, Jake had a definite sense of being sized up. The feeling reminded him of being seventeen years old and meeting a girl's parents for the first time.

Belatedly, he stepped forward and offered his hand. "You must be Mrs. Swanson."

She shook his hand, studying him with one more moment of frank curiosity before her neutral, polite facade fell back into place. "It's very nice to meet you. Mandy is back in tomorrow. We open at ten."

No information volunteered that wasn't strictly business. Jake had to applaud the professionalism, but now he missed the curiosity he'd glimpsed. If Mrs. Swanson had asked him any questions, it might have given him the opportunity to ask a few questions of his own.

Apparently Mandy hadn't mentioned him. His male ego stung a bit over that one. After all, this was the woman Mandy had her Christmas dinner with, and she'd told Jake about *that.*

Trying to wedge a foot into what appeared to be a rapidly closing door, he offered, "Mandy says some very nice things about you."

"I think highly of her, too. She's a lovely girl."

As Jake tried to read the woman's neutral tone, Mrs. Swanson's eyes wandered to an unlikely spot: the wall at the far right side of the shop. Jake saw nothing exceptional there, just a red-and-green array of Christmas stockings, collector plates and a couple of snowman prints.

"You have a beautiful store," Jake said. "Mandy tells me you stay pretty busy year-round?"

Her eyes returned to him. "We're slower now, to be sure," she said. "But we get a fair number of visitors, and sales are steady."

Business. A topic both of them felt at ease with. "How long have you had the store?"

"Nearly ten years. I bought it when I retired from teaching. The woman who sold it to me was about to close the shop altogether. It took a few years to bring the business up to where it is today."

"Congratulations. It's hard for small retailers to stay afloat, especially these days. And this store is so specialized—well, you're obviously doing something right."

"Oh, I can't take much credit." Mrs. Swanson smiled with an unexpected warmth, and Jake had a feeling he knew the secret of her success.

"Mandy?" he said.

"She made such a difference," Mrs. Swanson said. "She came in here fresh out of high school to ask about a job. I'd been running the store by myself, and I certainly wasn't planning to add any staff. But she was so sincere about wanting to work here, and it seemed—appropriate."

Mrs. Swanson's glance flickered to the far wall.

"She's been wonderful for business," she said. "She has something very special."

Her eyes returned to Jake, and that hint of sentiment vanished. "I make it a point to treat her well."

He didn't think he was imagining the message in her words as she looked at him.


"Merry Christmas," Mandy told the young couple as she sent them out the door with a carefully tissue-wrapped "Our First Christmas" ornament.

She liked seeing a husband and wife together in the store. A lot of men killed time elsewhere while their wives shopped here. And she loved the fact that she played a small part in helping them build a Christmas tradition.

Mrs. Swanson entered on the same jingle of bells on the door that saw the newlyweds out. Good. She could take lunch soon. The work day seemed longer than usual today, probably because she had a date with Jake tonight.

Mrs. Swanson stored her purse behind the counter. "A young man was here looking for you yesterday."

"Jake?" The name was out of Mandy's mouth before she thought about it.

"Yes, that was it. I told him you'd be back at work today. I didn't want to disturb you on your day off."

"Oh, that's all right." Trying for secrecy was a

lost cause. Trying for nonchalance instead, Mandy picked up the feather duster and cast her eyes around for some surface, any surface, that might need her attention. "He called me at home."

"Still busy with that housecleaning project?"

"I finally made some real headway." She'd constructed a tower of boxes in the hall closet that would put a New York skyscraper to shame, and she still hadn't been able to fit everything inside. She'd finally resorted to stuffing the last few boxes into her bedroom closet. "The house looks civilized now."

Mandy hoped she'd achieved the flavor of a mountain cabin, leaving out some of the pinecone ornaments and the swag of artificial evergreen underneath the fireplace mantel. The cardinal snow globe occupied a place of honor on the table in the entryway. In the kitchen, the Christmas village she'd painted over the years still decorated the tops of the cabinets.

A little bit of Christmas in every room. And she was exhausted.

Mrs. Swanson nodded. "It's good to be prepared for company."

*Expecting any?* might have been the unspoken question. Mandy decided not to hear it. She started toward the south wall with her duster, then belatedly changed direction, steering away from the space where the clippings had hung. She found a shelf of tiny blown-glass figurines and set to work.

But the missing clippings weren't so easily avoided.

"Take a little extra time on your lunch break today," Mrs. Swanson said. "That way you can pick up some new frames at the drugstore. Find a nice pair of matching ones."

The feather duster froze in Mandy's hand. Slowly, she turned to meet Mrs. Swanson's watchful eyes.

"It's still August," Mandy said. "Do you think there's any way we could give that display a little rest? Just until the Christmas season starts."

"Mandy." Her boss's voice was gentler than she expected. "You know that's a big part of what makes the store special."

"Sales are good. Especially for summer." Mrs. Swanson regarded her in silence. "I'll keep a running total," Mandy rushed on. "If we fall behind where we were last year, I'll hang them back up. And I'll put them up for good at the very beginning of November."

She didn't know whether Jake would be here until November, or if her secret could possibly hold till then. But she wanted as much time as she could buy.

Mrs. Swanson's eyes held hers. Her boss might have stopped teaching school ten years ago, but she obviously had no problem putting two and two together.

"Is he worth it?" Mrs. Swanson asked.

"I think he could be," Mandy said. "I just want a chance to find out."

That evening, November seemed far away.

Mandy stood beside Jake at the railing overlooking Tall Pine's tiny lake, holding a chocolate-dipped ice cream cone in one hand, Jake's hand in the other. They'd reached the pond just before sunset.

"This was a nice idea," Jake said.

Mandy didn't answer. She was involved in a race against time with her ice cream cone, trying to catch the vanilla that was leaking where the thin chocolate shell joined the cone.

After dinner, they'd gotten the cones at Penny's Ice Cream Shoppe on Evergreen Lane. From there, Mandy had brought Jake two blocks around the corner to the little park that encircled Prospect Lake, the town's fishing spot. The timing had been perfect; by seven-thirty, the sky had just begun to turn golden, the color reflected in the water. The handful of fishers on the other side of the lake were gathering up their gear before it got dark.

"I didn't even know you had a lake here," Jake said.

Mandy successfully navigated the ring of escaping vanilla before it reached her right hand. Her left hand stayed entwined with Jake's as their elbows rested on the railing—not very practical for eating ice cream, but his fingers laced through hers felt wonderful.

"It's more of a glorified duck pond." She looked down at the water a few feet below as some of the resident birds drifted closer. She ventured another bite out of the thin, creamy chocolate shell, releasing chaos as more vanilla escaped. She caught it with her tongue, trying to keep up. "They have to stock the lake with fish. It's man-made. If all the tourists knew about it, it'd be empty in a day."

"You do a lot of that up here, don't you?" Jake had already eaten his way through his ice cream's chocolate shell and was nearly down to the cone. "You like to keep things just small enough."

"It's nice." She ventured a glance away from her unstable, trickling ice cream to look at Jake, surprised to find him watching her rather than the lake. "What about you? You do a lot of trying to make things bigger."

"It's my job." He squeezed her fingers lightly. "And it's an unfortunate fact of life. If things don't grow, they have a tendency to die."

"We're not trying to turn into Mount Douglas."

Mandy chased another round of vanilla around her cone, now self-consciously aware of Jake's brown eyes following her progress.

"You couldn't. You don't have a ski resort."

"We don't get enough snow. We're not as high up." A big section of chocolate slid precariously down its melting vanilla base; Mandy barely caught it in her mouth before it fell to the ground.

"Exactly. So you need to make the most of what you do have."

"How can you advertise peace and quiet?" How could you successfully argue a point in the middle of eating a dipped cone? "If we get too busy, it won't be peaceful and quiet anymore."

"It's a delicate balance," he said. "But if you want your businesses to stay healthy . . ."

Jake trailed off, and she felt his gaze as she circled the melting vanilla before it reached her hand.

He said, "I'm going to have to help you with that in a minute, you know."

She glanced at Jake. His expression hinted at an interest in something more than ice cream. And somehow, he'd managed to get safely all the way down to his cone.

Mandy's face warmed. "You're better at multitasking than I am."

She lowered her eyes and concentrated on catching up with him. Jake seemed to be done with his discussion of controlled economic growth, at least for the moment.

As far as she could tell, he made sense. Maybe a little too much sense. It was hard to think of Tall Pine in terms of profit and loss. It was home, and while she knew tourists were good for business, she'd never thought very hard about what brought them here. Except for snow, and that was one thing no amount of planning could control.

As the sky deepened to a light orange, Mandy finished her ice cream, saving the last bit of cone for the ducks that still drifted lazily in the water. The birds had learned long ago that the presence of humans, sooner or later, added up to food. She tossed the piece into the lake and watched the ducks converge on the spot. The winner dipped its head into the water with a soft plunk. Others swam nearby, hoping there was more where that came from.

"Look what you started," Jake said. "I should have saved some of mine."

"Sometimes I come here with leftover bread."

"We could do that next time," he said.

*Next time.* The two simple words had a sweet ring to her ears. How quickly all this was starting to feel normal. Like something that was meant to be.

Two other, unwelcome words crowded into her brain: *Tell him.*

She shivered, and Jake put his arm around her shoulders, shutting out a chilly breeze that was just starting to creep past the barrier of Mandy's sweater. But that wasn't what had made her shiver.

She gazed out at the water, the ducks and geese on its surface beginning to darken into silhouettes. "How long will you be here, Jake?" Her voice sounded wobbly to her own ears, less casual than she'd intended.

"Well, your city council might decide that."

*"Town* council," she corrected him. "We call Tall Pine a town, not a city. Don't forget that."

"Thanks." He rested his cheek on top of her head. "Well, if the council gives me the go-ahead, there's a lot to do to see a project like this through. Usually six or seven months. If they say no—"

The thought set off little flames in her stomach, tickling at the bottom of her ribs.

He sighed. "I don't know. I've never had a project turned down before. But I don't plan on giving up without a fight."

She dreaded having Jake leave. But she was almost as afraid to have him stay long enough to find out her whole story. So far, things were perfect, and part of her wanted to leave them that way.

She shivered again, and Jake brought his other arm across her waist, encircling her. It shut out the cold air wonderfully. It even did a little for the chill she felt inside.

"It's getting colder," he said.

Mandy felt the beginnings of goose bumps on Jake's bare arms. Belatedly, she realized that in his short-sleeved polo shirt, he must feel the chill in the air more than she did. "You need a jacket."

"I brought a couple with me. Thing is, they're all suit jackets. Someone told me this was Southern California, and this was summertime."

"Someone should have told you it's colder up here in the mountains." Even with Jake's arms around her, Mandy could feel the breeze from the lake starting to cut through the knit of her sweater. She huddled a little closer, this time trying to share some of her warmth with him. "And it probably doesn't help that you're full of ice cream."

"Good point." He kissed the top of her head. "You could talk me into watching the sunset from the truck."

As they reached the parking lot on Evergreen Lane, they saw a pretty blond woman with two little girls, even blonder. The woman was sliding open the door to the backseat of a family van parked next to Jake's truck.

The bigger girl, about four years old, turned toward Mandy. "It's the Santa lady!"

"Santa lady?" their mother echoed.

Tongue-tied, Mandy took in the blond trio now staring at her. The older girl's eyes were brown, like her mother's. The younger sister's eyes were a blend of blue and green. Such pretty variations on a theme. She remembered the similarities and the differences. . . .

"You were at Christmas in July, weren't you?" Mandy said.

The girls nodded, their eyes even bigger than before.

"I met them at our sidewalk sale," Mandy told their mother. "I work at the Christmas store. They were there with their daddy."

And, of course, she'd told them about Santa. Aware of Jake standing behind her, Mandy's heart hammered.

"July," the mother said. "It must have been when I was out of town at my sister's."

The older girl tugged at her mother's blouse. "Mom, she told us one night she—"

"Your name is Bailey, right?" Mandy interrupted.

Bailey nodded, pleased to be remembered, and forgot to finish what she was going to say.

"And Rosie." Mandy turned her eyes to the smaller girl, about two years old.

Their mother stepped forward. "We just moved here at the beginning of the summer. I'm Renee."

She shook the woman's hand. "I'm Mandy. This is Jake."

Jake shook Renee's hand. "Nice to meet you." He looked down at the girls, who hovered shyly near their mother. "And Bailey and Rosie. Nice to meet you, too."

And they left, before Bailey remembered what she'd been about to say.

# Chapter 6

Mandy turned the key in the front door, letting Jake into her house for the first time.

They'd finished watching the sunset from the front seat of Jake's rented pickup, followed by kisses that had made her heady. That headiness might have accounted for Mandy's next idea: when they didn't find a movie that appealed to them at the multiplex, she'd invited him to her house to watch a DVD from her collection.

She dropped her keys on the floor as they stepped into the entryway, nearly clunking her head into Jake's as they both bent to pick them up.

"Here you go." Jake's fingers brushed hers as he handed her the keys.

Mandy stepped away and switched on the lights. The living room was immediately to the right of the tiled entryway, and she tried to see it through his eyes. To her, it still felt sparse compared to the way it had looked a few days ago. Was the pine garland hanging from the mantelpiece too Christmasy for summer?

"It's warm in here." Jake sounded relieved.

In contrast to the mountain breeze outside, the house still held the warmth it had built up from the afternoon sun. As Mandy started to take off her sweater, Jake helped her, sliding the sleeves down over her arms in a gesture that, perversely, set off yet another kind of shiver.

*That* was what she hadn't thought about when she invited him back to her house. The possible implications of being alone with him, at night, in her home, hadn't hit her until they reached the front porch. Standing close to him now, completely alone, it was suddenly impossible to think of anything else.

As he slipped her sweater off, he kissed her lightly. And handed her the sweater.

She thought it might be his way of saying, *You can trust me.*

Mandy exhaled a breath she hadn't realized she was holding and debated what to do with the sweater. She decided against opening the precariously loaded hall closet. She draped it over the back of the sofa instead.

Jake turned to survey the living room. "So, this is the house you grew up in."

"This is it."

"It feels like it." She gave him a puzzled look.

"I mean, it feels like you. I mean—" He grinned ruefully.

She tried to remember if she'd seen Jake this tongue-tied before. It hadn't occurred to Mandy that nerves could work on both sides.

"'Comfortable' isn't a very flattering word," he said. "Would you settle for 'homey'?"

"It'll do. How about some coffee?"

"Sounds great."

She started toward the kitchen, then stopped. "You can have a seat and make yourself comfortable," she said. "Or if you want to take a look at the movie choices . . ." She crossed the living room to the cabinet beside the television set and pulled it open to expose four rows of wide shelves. There were shelves in the doors, too.

"Impressive." Jake's eyes took on a gleam, and he crouched on the floor for a better view. "Are they organized any special way?"

"Sort of." Starting to feel more normal, Mandy crouched alongside him. "Classic dramas." She pointed a finger along the rows of shelves as she talked. "Contemporary dramas. Thrillers. Romantic comedies. Musicals . . ." She passed her hand in front of the door on the right. "And the very top shelf—comfort food. My all-time favorites. Those aren't broken up by category. And nothing's alphabetized."

"I'm surprised at you."

"Okay, so how are yours organized at home?"

"Easy. They're a mess."

She laughed and stood up to go and make the coffee.

A movie collection, Jake decided, was a window to the soul.

He started with that top shelf. *Casablanca,* of course. He was pleased to find *To Kill a Mockingbird* there too. *Breakfast at Tiffany's* and *The Princess Bride* were obvious, female-friendly favorites. But there were a few surprises.

"*The Godfather* is comfort food?" he called out to the kitchen.

"Only the first one. But the other two have to go with it, because I didn't want to separate them."

"You're a regular Library of Congress." He stood and joined Mandy in the kitchen.

It didn't look like she'd made any progress on the coffee yet. As he entered, she was transferring glasses from the sink to the dishwasher. She closed the dishwasher quickly.

"Something's fishy," he said.

She turned with a start. "What?"

"I don't see any Christmas movies."

She grinned. "There wasn't room. I've got a whole separate box for those. They're put away with the Christmas decorations."

Jake folded his arms. "How many?"

She inclined her head, considering. "About forty. But that's because I'm selective. Did you pick anything out?"

"Help me narrow it down. I can't handle the responsibility."

"You saw the favorites shelf."

"That's a pretty broad selection. What are you in the mood for?"

"Well . . ." She opened a cabinet and brought out a can of coffee. "*Ghost* might be my all-time favorite, but I'm not sure if you'd care for it. I've been trying to get Mrs. Swanson to watch it for years. She can't get past the basic idea. She thinks, if it couldn't happen, what's the point in watching it?"

"That rules out a lot of movies. Especially if you count *Pretty Woman*."

She started judiciously measuring coffee into the filter basket of the coffeemaker. As she brought out another scoop of grounds, she eyed the size of the mound that crowned over the top of the scoop, then shook it to level it a little more before she dropped it into the filter.

So painstaking . . . and so irresistible.

Jake stepped behind her and spoke just above her ear. "*Ghost* is fine with me," he said. "Believe it or not, I've never seen it. Something about Demi Moore being haunted by her husband?"

He smoothed her hair back, tucking it behind her ear. A delicate gold pine tree earring dangled from her earlobe. It shimmered when his fingers brushed it.

Mandy measured out another scoop of coffee, not so precisely this time. "I can't concentrate if you do that."

"That's the idea." He moved his lips downward and kissed her ear. She gave a little shudder that triggered a matching shudder of his own. She relaxed against him. He closed his eyes and buried his face against the side of her neck, drinking in the scent of whatever it was she wore, that delicious hint of spice. For several exquisite moments, he didn't move, just standing there with her, hearing her breathe.

Then she stepped away and carried the coffee carafe to the sink to fill it with water.

"Seriously, though," she said. "Have you ever wondered what you'd do in a situation like that?"

He was crushed that she'd kept her train of thought. He'd certainly lost his. "Like what?"

"If you were a character in a movie like that. With ghosts, or angels, or . . . whatever." Her tone was offhand. Her back was turned, so he couldn't see her expression. "How would you handle it?"

"Handle what?"

"What if you saw something you thought was impossible? You don't believe in—say, ghosts, right?"

He blinked. "Right."

She brought back the water, poured it into the coffeemaker and switched it on. "So what would you do if you walked into your kitchen and a ghost was standing by the sink?"

She'd left him far behind. "I guess I'd figure it was my imagination."

"But what would you *do*? They're standing right there in front of you."

"This is a weird conversation, Mandy."

"Come on. Humor me. Think about it."

"Okay." He tilted his head back and squinted up at the ceiling. "If I could see through them, I'd know it was my imagination, or that I was dreaming. And I'd go back to bed. If they looked solid . . . I'd probably try talking to them and find out if they had the wrong house. But first I'd grab a baseball bat."

It sounded reasonable to him. She didn't seem satisfied. Jake had no idea what kind of an answer she was looking for.

"What would *you* do?" he asked.

"I think about it sometimes." She watched the stream of coffee trickling into the clear carafe. "And I think . . . I think I might believe my own eyes."

She looked at Jake again. The coffeemaker chugged out its brewing noises.

He risked a smile. "Mandy, are you trying to tell me your kitchen is haunted?"

"No." She returned his smile with a much smaller one of her own. "I was just kidding around."

He had a feeling he'd failed an exam of some sort. And he wasn't so sure that Mandy hadn't seen a ghost in her kitchen.

"Don't get me wrong," he said. "I love fantasy. I guess I just think if there really were ghosts, you'd hear about a lot more people seeing them. There'd be more evidence."

How had this turned into a debate over paranormal experiences? He felt a little uneasy. He'd rather argue over which movie to watch.

"It doesn't mean it doesn't make a good story," he added. "I told you, the old monster movies are some of my favorites."

She was staring at the coffee again, but the pot wasn't even half full. "Come on. Let's take another look." She led him back into the living room and leaned over the movie cabinet. "What haven't you seen in here?"

Apparently, *Ghost* was off the table. He joined her in front of the shelves. "Not a lot, except for the musicals. And those would be a tough sell for me."

"Men." She shook her head, but her tone seemed

amiable. Whatever that conversation had been about, it was over. At least, as far as he could tell.

They settled on *Breakfast at Tiffany's,* and Mandy returned to the kitchen. "How do you like your coffee?"

"Black."

"I thought so."


During the movie, Mandy's mind wandered as she tried to imagine how Jake could ever accept her experience with Santa Claus.

*Ghost* hadn't been a good comparison, anyway. Mandy didn't believe in ghosts either. But a movie was a movie, and life was life. Jake could cheerfully suspend disbelief for a reanimated monster. Everyday life was a different story.

Like most people, Jake lived in a realistic world. And like most people, when he heard who Mandy had seen, he'd never believe her.

They'd darkened the room for the movie, but in the light cast by the glow of the screen, Mandy could still see the fireplace. *Right there.* She'd seen him.

Jake would be more receptive if she told him Steven Spielberg had dropped by her house.

She sighed and rested her head on his shoulder. He responded by curling his arm around her. And once again, it felt natural and right. Maybe she was underestimating him.

*I want to keep this.*

With the comfortable weight of Jake's arm around her shoulders, at last Mandy focused on the movie and let *Breakfast at Tiffany's* work its magic.

# Chapter 7

He was finally starting to acclimate.

Jake jogged to the rear of his hotel and walked the rest of the way to the front entrance, so he wouldn't be flat-out huffing and puffing when he made his entrance in the lobby. By his best calculations, he'd made it a mile today. At home, that would have been pitiful. Here, it was progress.

He'd persisted with his morning running routine since he got to Tall Pine, but the change in altitude had been a blow to his ego. Less than ten minutes into his first attempt, his lungs had turned into a small, achy box in his chest, without room to catch enough oxygen. Today, the thinner mountain air still seared his lungs. But at the same time, it felt clean and invigorating.

The cold air would have been just the thing to clear his head, if a certain petite brunette didn't keep nudging at the edge of his thoughts. It didn't feel like a bad thing. But it wasn't like him. In the past, he'd spent too many dates letting business strategies and ledger columns intrude on his thoughts. Now Mandy was following him around, and she didn't even know it. *Who needs to see ghosts?*

Maybe once he could run another mile, he'd be better able to focus. In the meantime, there was business at hand. Today was Friday, and he'd managed to get through a whole week without taking any serious forward steps to start the ball rolling on the hotel. Fact-finding was all well and good, but the fact was, he'd been stalling and he knew it. That had to stop today.

With a few more deep breaths, he crossed the long front porch in front of The Evergreen Inn. A few chunky wooden chairs waited for anyone who'd care to take a seat and watch the quiet side street just off Evergreen Lane. If the hotel owners were to widen that porch and add a few tables, they'd have an area that really invited guests to linger.

Not that it was up to him to tell them their business. In fact, before long, he'd be setting up a business to compete with theirs. He was starting to feel almost guilty about it. Silly. He'd never felt guilty staying at a Red Roof Inn while he set up a Regal Hotel, and they were much closer to being in the same bracket. This would be apples and oranges. *Cooperative competition,* he reminded himself.

But as he walked in and smiled at the desk

clerk, a sixtyish woman who ran the place with her husband, it didn't feel that way. He'd played his cards close to the vest longer than he should, and he hoped it didn't come back to bite him.

The woman behind the desk—Phyllis, that was her name—returned his smile with a slightly puzzled one of her own. He'd been here too long to be a typical tourist, especially with no wife or family in tow. But he probably didn't look much like their usual business traveler, either. Or did they get any of those here? Probably not.

Before he put in for Regal's permit, he'd better talk to her. But not before he'd had a shower.

He just hoped, after he told her, that their little continental breakfast of self-serve cereal and wrapped Danishes would still be open to him.

"You were right," he told Mandy as they sat down at a table inside the Pine 'n' Dine. "Tall Pine is different."

He'd grabbed her out of The North Pole for an early lunch, one final effort to forestall his next step on the hotel project. Going to the town hall to set things in motion would be like diving headfirst into chilly water.

"How'd Phyllis take it when you told her?"

"She thanked me for being honest with her. But she looked wounded." There wasn't a waiter or waitress in sight. Jake picked up two menus from the wire rack at the side of their tabletop and handed one to Mandy. "I felt like I should buy her a basket of fruit or something."

"You did the right thing."

"It's not like I had a lot of choice. If she didn't hear it from me, she'd hear it from someone else, and that would be worse." He laid his menu flat in front of him and ran a hand through his hair. "It's never been like this. It's always been business. All of a sudden I'm starting to feel like I'm messing with somebody's livelihood."

"Business is always somebody's livelihood," Mandy said.

"Yeah. Mine." He picked up a cracker packet, realized he didn't want it, and set it down. "I come in, I get the job done, I make a living. I don't think I've left a bunch of DoubleTree carcasses behind me. The little hotels here—I don't think we'd put them out of business either. But I can see where they'd be worried." He passed his hand through his hair again and looked at her ruefully. "You don't think I'm Satan, do you?"

"Of course not." She smiled across the table at him. "Snidely Whiplash, maybe. But not Satan."

"Thanks."

"You're a good guy, Jake." Mandy's blue eyes went serious. "That's why you're worried about it."

He grinned weakly. "I'm worried about going down in flames. Nothing too unselfish about that."

Mandy ran a finger lightly over his hand on the table. "It'll be okay."

Her tone said she wasn't sure just how. But somehow, hearing her say it meant a lot. Jake took a deep breath, counted to twenty, and shifted his attention to the menu.

The pictures and prices were just starting to make sense to him when a waitress arrived and set two glasses of water on the table.

"Hey," she said. "It's Mandy Claus."

Jake chuckled. He hadn't heard that one before. To his surprise, Mandy flinched.

"Hi, Sherry," she said.

The waitress looked about Mandy's age, with strawberry-red hair that almost certainly wasn't her natural color. Sherry's eyes went to Jake with roughly triple the amount of curiosity he'd gotten used to in Tall Pine. Then she switched back to Mandy. "How are things at The North Pole?"

"Business as usual." Mandy's voice was cheery as she smiled back at the waitress, but her smile seemed just a little too tight.

Sherry took their order, her gaze lingering on Jake. Maybe she had a penchant for playing up to other women's boyfriends. Mandy didn't introduce them, and her attention stayed fixed on Sherry until the redhead walked away.

"Mandy Claus," he repeated after Sherry disappeared into the kitchen. "That's a new one."

"It gets old after a while."

*Older than Christmas carols year-round?* Jake wondered. "You didn't mind when that little girl called you the Santa lady."

Her cheeks reddened. "That's different. She was a little girl."

There was some kind of undercurrent here. Jake took a guess. "Was she in your class in school?" He inclined his head toward the kitchen.

"All the way through." Mandy took a drink from her water glass.

"Want me to pull her hair for you?"

It got a laugh out of her, which was what he wanted. And of course, it was a joke. But if Sherry had given Mandy a bad time in school, Jake found he didn't feel as kindly toward her.

Mandy shook her head. "Sherry's okay, really. I just . . ." She leaned forward and rested her elbows on the table, her chin in her hands.

"What's it like?" she asked. "To go someplace where nobody knows you? You do it all the time."

She looked so earnest. Even wistful.

Jake thought about it. "It does give you a kind of freedom," he said. "You start out fresh. Nobody knows about your old mistakes. On the other hand, you have to keep reestablishing yourself, and that takes some work. It can get tiring. When I was a kid, I hated it. We moved around a lot when I was younger. My dad would get a better job, a promotion, and there'd be a new house, a new school, a new city. By the time I got the hang of it, we settled down. I was thirteen."

"So, staying in one place was better?"

"Well, sure. When you're a kid you want some continuity. It's tough leaving friends right when you get to know them. But it was a learning experience. I think it's made it easier for me to learn my way around when I come to a new town."

She studied him and shook her head. "Starting over in a new place sounds exciting. But it's hard for me to even picture it."

"What's it like for you? Living in the same place all your life?"

"It's hard to say." Mandy jiggled her water glass and watched the ice cubes shift. "I don't have anything to compare it to. And it's probably a lot different if it's a bigger place. Here, I know just about everybody, and they know all about me." She rolled her eyes and took a drink.

"There've got to be some pluses, right? Or you wouldn't still be here."

"Maybe the pluses are the same as the minuses." She set down her glass. "People know you, so you don't have to explain a lot about yourself. But they've got this idea of who you are—" She lifted her shoulders in a shrug. "It's comfortable, and it's limiting."

He couldn't imagine Mandy wanting to be any different. "What would you change if you could?"

"That's just it. I don't know." She folded her arms around herself. "I tried once. After my mom died. I thought, *What's keeping me here?* Aside from the fact that I didn't know the first thing about selling a house. So I tried an experiment."

He waited for her to go on.

Mandy said, "You know, I've never told anybody about this." Her eyes drifted past him. "I took a couple days off, and I drove up to Mount Douglas. I stayed at a hotel, I drove around, I shopped, and I didn't see a single soul who knew me for three days. I wanted to at least try it out, see what it might feel like to live somewhere else. Even if I decided not to leave, I thought it would be a nice break."

An uncharacteristic frown formed between her brows. "It was *awful.* I felt invisible. Lost. Like I'd been dropped on another planet. Everything was foreign. And that was just Mount Douglas. Same mountains, same trees . . . not exactly the big city." She rattled the ice in her glass. "So I came back here, and here's where I've been ever since. It's home." She shrugged, and a little weight seemed to fall off her shoulders with the movement. "It's

**101**

beautiful up here. I don't have to explain myself or introduce myself, and there are a lot of nice people. The worst thing is, they know everything I've ever done."

Mandy turned toward the kitchen, and sure enough, Sherry was headed their way with their plates.

"Now's your chance," Jake whispered. "Hair-pulling?"

Mandy bit her lip, and for a minute Jake thought she might giggle. But as Sherry set down their plates, the two women exchanged glances again. Jake would have given a lot to have a lesson in female telepathy, because something unspoken was going on here.

Sherry straightened, directing her question toward Mandy. "Anything else I can get for you?"

Mandy shook her head.

"We're great," Jake said. "Thanks."

Sherry smiled and turned away.

"You know, I can think of two things wrong with your experiment," Jake said.

Mandy contemplated him over her sandwich.

"You say you felt lost," he said. "That's because, number one, you went there without any real purpose. I've got a job that sends me places. I've got something to do when I get there. Number two, whenever I leave home, I know I've got a place to come back to. Even if I hardly ever see it." He grinned. "And, confession time. In Pennsylvania, I'm just twenty minutes away from my parents. So I've even got access to good home cooking."

"You mean, you're spoiled rotten."

"Amen."

Jake picked up his sandwich. *Spoiled* was right. Mandy lived in the same home she'd grown up in. But there was no family to come home to.

*I never thought about how good I have it.*


Fortified by lunch, Jake set out on his next order of business.

From the outside, the Tall Pine town hall had a rustic charm. Instead of the usual concrete and pillars, the A-frame building reminded Jake of a Swiss chalet, trimmed with the natural woodwork that seemed so popular around here. Decidedly unbureaucratic.

Inside, though, the illusion gave way to the usual faceless lobby, big for the sake of being big. This was a government building, all right. It should have made him feel more at home; he'd done this a lot of times by now.

He followed the signs to the permit office and passed through the glass door into a room with no-nonsense gray carpet and windowed counters. Squaring his shoulders, Jake walked up to the first window, where a fiftyish woman sat. Her hairstyle reminded him of Mandy's employer. Sculpted waves didn't seem to have gone out of style in Tall Pine.

Jake noted her name plaque on the window as he walked up: MRS. CASSANDRA CASSIDY.

Showtime.

"Hello, Mrs. Cassidy. I'm Jake Wyndham. I'd like to find out the procedure for opening a new business here in town."

The woman behind the counter donned a pair of black reading glasses and slid her keyboard toward her. "Purpose of the business?"

"It's a hotel."

"Name of the owner?"

"Regal Hotels."

Her fingers froze over the keyboard. If there had been anyone else nearby, Jake was sure his or her head would have swiveled around. In his mind, he heard a whiskey shot glass fall to the floor of his imaginary old Western tavern and shatter.

"I see." She recovered gamely and peered at him over the plastic rims of her glasses. "Use of the land will have to be reviewed and approved at a public meeting of the town council." It sounded like she had the regulations memorized. "Any businesses within five miles will be entitled to give their input."

"That's got to be most of the town."

She nodded. "This is a small community, Mr. . . . ."

"Wyndham," he reminded her, throwing in his best smile. "Jake."

"Mr. Wyndham. And a project of this nature would have a sizable impact on the community."

He wondered if she left the five-dollar words behind the desk when she left work. But her voice wasn't unkind. Her eyes betrayed a hint of the "do you know what you're up against?" he'd heard from Mandy the day they met.

"I understand." He kept his smile in place. "What do I do first?"

"The next town council meeting is—" She flipped up the page of a small wall calendar hanging from the side of her cubicle. "September eighteenth."

"You're kidding." He cleared his throat. "I mean, that's surprising."

"It meets the third Wednesday of every month."

A city council that only met once a month? Jake was starting to wonder how Regal had found Tall Pine on the map.

"I see. Is it possible for me to have that item placed on the agenda now?"

Mrs. Cassidy reached for her keyboard again, and Jake thought he saw one corner of her mouth turn upward. As if she knew she was helping him fire the next shot heard around the world.

\* \* \*

That evening, after work, Mandy didn't get into her car to drive home. She made a beeline for the diner.

At just after five p.m., it was already busier than it had been at lunchtime. The Friday-night tourist dinner trade was coming in. The stand-up sign in the waiting area had been turned around from PLEASE SEAT YOURSELF to PLEASE WAIT TO BE SEATED.

Mandy walked past the sign. She wasn't here to sit.

Sherry was at the back of the restaurant, pushing through the swinging door that led into the kitchen. Mandy followed her in, ignoring the faint protest of a young brunette waitress behind her.

"Sherry," Mandy said.

Grabbing two plates from the cook, the redhead wheeled around. "Hey, you're not supposed to be—"

When she saw who had followed her, she fell silent. Mandy felt a twinge of guilt for bursting in at the dinner rush, but this couldn't wait.

She licked her lips. "Sherry, I know you're busy, and I won't take a lot of your time. But I need a big favor."

The other waitress came in, tearing an order from her pad, and Mandy stepped aside. After the girl gave the order to the cook, Sherry handed her two plates to the brunette.

"Tiffany, could you take these to table four? I owe you one."

Bewildered, Tiffany took the plates and left.

"So," Sherry said, eyes gleaming with curiosity. "Does this have anything to do with Mr. Tall, Dark and Gorgeous?"

"This is serious."

"I guess so."

"Please don't say anything. About Santa Claus."

Sherry blinked. "What?"

"The Mandy Claus crack, Sherry. He doesn't know about it. He's here on business, maybe not for very long—" Mandy cleared her throat. "Just don't tell him I saw Santa."

"So now you're trying to keep it a secret?" Sherry asked. "Good luck with that."

"Sherry, it's the first time *any* guy hasn't known."

"He's going to find out sooner or later," Sherry said. "What are you going to do then?"

"I'll cross that bridge when I come to it."

Sherry frowned. "Don't you think the longer you wait, the worse it'll be?"

Mandy had thought about it. Constantly. Sensible Jake, with his warm smile and his facts and figures. Wondering which side of him would win out.

Tiffany entered and handed an order slip to the chef. "You've got two more customers at your tables," she told Sherry.

Sherry nodded. "Be right there."

"I don't think it matters how long it takes him to find out," Mandy said. "I think the reaction's going to be the same no matter what."

"You think he'd bail out on you? Maybe you should give him a little more credit."

"Sherry, there's a reason I've never dated much. The odds that he'd really believe me—"

Picking up two loaded plates from the counter, Sherry turned around, eyebrows raised.

"You mean you're holding out for a guy who believes in Santa Claus?" Sherry shook her head. "Sweetie, you're going to have a long wait."

Sherry elbowed her way through the swinging doors, leaving Mandy standing alone in the kitchen. The cook looked at her questioningly, as if to say, *Are you going to grab a plate or get out?*

She walked outside. It was still broad daylight at five-thirty. Usually, by late August, Mandy enjoyed watching for the days to get shorter, sniffing the air for the first breath of fall. Colder air and stiffer breezes brought the promise of Christmas.

This year, the thought of Christmas brought a mixture of anticipation and dread. It was the time of year she lived for. It brought more customers to the shop, more children to tell her story to. . . .

And Mrs. Swanson would hold her to her promise to hang the newspaper clippings up again.

If Jake was here for the Christmas season,

there was no way she'd be able to hide the truth from him.

Sherry was probably right. Mandy should come clean now. For good or for bad, the moment she'd seen Santa Claus had formed a huge part of who she was. If Jake didn't know about that, he didn't really know her at all.

But if the hotel project didn't go through, she wouldn't have to deal with it. Plenty of other people had summer flings, she reminded herself. At this early stage that was probably all she meant to Jake. He knew, hotel or no hotel, that he'd be leaving eventually, heading clear back to the other side of the country.

She didn't want Jake to fail. And she didn't want him to leave.

Mandy breathed in deeply, trying to tell if she detected any scent of fall at all.

Her only answer was the familiar scent of pine trees. She lived surrounded by them twelve months a year, but their aroma still carried an inextricable link to Christmas.

# Chapter 8

Word got around fast.

By Sunday afternoon, every establishment Jake walked into felt like that old Western saloon. From the filling station where he gassed up the truck to the little market where he picked up groceries for his kitchenette, curious stares followed him.

When he stopped at the Pine 'n' Dine for coffee Monday morning and Sherry asked him how the hotel business was, he figured Tall Pine had been officially saturated with the news.

Jake met the stares with smiles and started introducing himself. People were polite, even friendly, but he could sense an invisible shield in front of them. He reminded himself of how they must feel. They thought he was coming here to change the town, rather than make the most of what they had. He decided to make his initial goal a modest one: to show the people of Tall Pine that he didn't bite.

The biggest surprise was Mandy. Whenever she

was with him, the glances that followed him went up exponentially. He'd thought she might shrink away or try to distance herself from him, but if anything, she stood closer, meeting curious looks with direct eye contact. He didn't see her make any attempt to hide their relationship.

Labor Day weekend brought the Tall Pine Fall Festival, and Jake was pleased to see Phyllis's hotel flooded to the gills. Just up the road, the Tall Pine Lodge also boasted a *No Vacancy* sign by Friday morning. Good news for them, good news for Regal. It showed there was plenty of business to go around. He texted the home office with news about the crowd.

So far, his regional director was being patient about the delay caused by the town council meeting. Mark knew Jake could keep up on the rest of his work online and over the phone, and Jake had pointed out that he could use the extra time to get better acquainted with the people of Tall Pine, especially the powers-that-be. So, while Mandy manned a table for a sidewalk sale at The North Pole, Jake dove into the thick of the Fall Festival.

Sidewalk sales lined both sides of Evergreen Lane, but the event culminated at the town square, where the lane dead-ended. Here, more tables and booths were set up, including a small section of vendors holding a miniature craft fair. But most of the booths in the town square represented Tall

Pine's community organizations: the chamber of commerce, the local Rotary and Kiwanis clubs, veterans' groups—even a dunking booth for the mayor.

Jake wasn't going to touch *that* one.

He smiled, shook hands and mingled. By late afternoon he'd met four of the six members of the town council, who greeted him with carefully neutral smiles. This wasn't the venue to pitch the project, and Jake knew it. He just made sure they knew who he was.

By four p.m., he worked his way back down Evergreen Lane to pick Mandy up at The North Pole shortly before the store closed. He got there just in time to help Mandy and Mrs. Swanson drag in the two long tables from the sidewalk sale.

"How'd you do today?" he asked as they set the table down near the store's front windows, where they could easily bring it out to the sidewalk again in the morning.

"Busy," Mandy said, straightening her red top. The tip of her nose bore a trace of sunburn from her hours outside, and her dark hair fell around her face, slightly tousled. It looked as if she hadn't had much time to stop today.

"It was our busiest day this month," Mrs. Swanson said.

September had, of course, barely started. Her

expression remained a total deadpan. Jake was pretty sure she was kidding, but not sure enough to risk laughing.

Instead, he turned to Mandy and held out the simple brown gift bag he'd carried in with him. "I brought you something."

He could have waited until they got out to the truck, but for some reason he was anxious to have her see it.

"Early Christmas present," he added.

Mandy had given him a light blue windbreaker earlier this week, passing it off as an early Christmas gift. He'd spotted his little surprise—a bauble, Mandy would probably call it—on a craft table along Evergreen Lane, and he hadn't been able to leave it behind. Part of it was that she'd caught him unawares when she gave him the windbreaker, and he welcomed the chance to give something in return. Part of it was simply that he'd thought of her immediately when he saw it.

She accepted the bag, her smile a little tentative. "You didn't have to do that."

"It's nothing huge. It just made me think of you, so I grabbed it."

As she held the little package with red and green tissue paper poking up out of it, he could see the glint of temptation in her eyes. "You want me to open it right now?" She glanced self-consciously toward Mrs. Swanson, who stood at a discreet distance.

"Unless you want to wait till December."

Her smile grew. After another fleeting moment of hesitation, she set the bag on the table, plucked out the tissue and reached inside. She fished out a little handcrafted wooden sign with a wire hanger on top.

It read WELCOME, SANTA in green letters, painted with white polka dots to look like old-fashioned fabric. A red Santa hat had been cut into the top left corner at a jaunty angle, as though its wearer had hung it there casually after a long night's work.

Mandy's reaction wasn't what he expected. She raised a hand to her mouth in surprise.

He tried to read her expression. The gift didn't match the windbreaker in size or value, he knew, but . . .

"I guess you already have a lot of Christmas things," Jake said. "I just saw it at one of the craft tables, and it reminded me of you."

Her hand still in front of her mouth, she asked, "Do you like it?"

He nodded cautiously. "Do you?"

She lowered her hand to reveal her smile, along with a slight flush to her cheeks. "I did when I made it."

Mandy turned over the sign and showed him the

initials written in red marker behind the Santa hat: *MLR*.

Jake stared. "You're kidding."

What were the odds? The craft table had held dozens of pieces of bric-a-brac, some of them Christmas decorations, some not. This had been the one that jumped out at him.

"She made those after Christmas a year or two ago when I gave her a Skilsaw," Mrs. Swanson said. "We brought them out for the craft fair."

Jake studied the handwritten initials. "So, what does the *L* stand for?"

"Lee. That was my grandmother's name."

She flipped the ornament back over, and Jake took another look at Mandy's handiwork. He didn't know anything about the artistic nuance of craft painting, but . . . "You did a nice job. You should sell those here."

Mandy pointed to a little stack of signs at the far end of the sale table they'd carried in.

"We kept some here," she said, "and I gave some to Linda for her consignment table."

"Well, there goes your profit," Jake said. "I went through a middleman."

Mandy chuckled and, standing on tiptoe, crooked her arm around his neck for a short hug. Right in front of Mrs. Swanson. Jake felt absurdly pleased.

"Now I've got one to keep for myself," she said. "Thank you."

"You know, I just realized," Jake said, casting his eyes over the store, "you don't have much Santa Claus merchandise in here."

Mrs. Swanson drifted away toward the counter, while Mandy frowned thoughtfully.

"You're right. We don't order too many Santa things," Mandy said. "Maybe it's because he's so hard to get right."

"Come again?"

"So much of the Santa stuff you see—I don't know. His suit is such a bright red, it looks sort of fake. And his smile . . . It's hard to explain. It can look kind of corny."

Jake's eyebrows went up. "Mandy, I'm surprised at you. You almost sound like the Grinch. Don't you believe in Santa Claus?"

Mrs. Swanson made a sound as she retrieved her purse from behind the counter. Something like a strangled cough.

Mandy turned nearly as red as the decorations she'd been talking about. "I believe in Santa as much as anybody. It's just that he's . . . magic. And that's hard to put on a plate or a pillow."

Jake tried to follow her point. "So you feel like it's better to leave him to the imagination."

"Something like that." She fingered the hat at the corner of the little ornament. "That's why I didn't try to do the face."

"Well, now that that's settled—" Mrs. Swanson

**116**

passed them on her way to the door. "Good night, you two."

Yes, Jake strongly suspected the woman had a sense of humor.

"Well, Christmas girl," Jake said, "shall we go celebrate the unofficial end of summer?"

They reached the town square in under five minutes. The flavor of the festival had shifted in the short time Jake had been gone. With evening approaching, the focus was changing from crafts to food. Most vendors were putting away their wares for the day, and the aroma of barbecued meat grew more enticing as the late afternoon breeze carried it along.

With Mandy beside him, the Fall Festival became less about making contacts and more about enjoying the moment. Any more schmoozing could wait until tomorrow.

A stage had been set up in the center of the town square lawn, and strains of an acoustic band tuning up reached them as they picked up their barbecued sandwiches. They headed for the folding chairs set up on the grass—only a hundred or so, Jake noticed, as if they'd planned for a modest crowd.

As they walked between the seats, Jake noticed a tall, sandy-haired man standing at the end of a row, watching them. Mandy changed direction and doubled back to one of the rows they'd already

**117**

passed, closer to the stage but farther from their viewer.

Jake hadn't seen anything like that since their first night at the movie theater. His first thought was the same one he'd had then. "Ex-boyfriend?"

He wondered if she'd play dumb, but she laughed. "Scotty Leroux? No way."

Jake took another look at his lanky potential rival. He knew male appreciation when he saw it, and he couldn't exactly blame the guy for the look he was sending Mandy's way. He also couldn't help feeling smug.

She pulled Jake away. "Come on."

He let her draw him to a pair of seats she apparently deemed a suitable distance away. A little farther forward, so it would give Scotty Leroux a view of the backs of their heads. They sat down.

"What's the deal?" Jake asked.

"He's the one who came up with 'Mandy Claus,'" she said. "I've been hearing it since fourth grade."

Jake frowned. "Fourth grade? You couldn't have been working at the Christmas store in the fourth grade."

"Never mind."

Jake cast a quick glance over his shoulder. This time the other man looked away.

Jake said. "You may not care for him, but he sure likes you."

Mandy shook her head.

**118**

"Come on. Why is that so hard for you to believe? I can tell from where I'm sitting."

"You don't know him."

"No, but I know guys, because I happen to be one. You know how a first-grader shows a girl he likes her? He punches her in the arm. By fourth grade, it gets a little more subtle. He still can't admit he likes her, so he teases her."

Mandy shook her head again and bit into her sandwich.

"What I still don't get," Jake said, "is how 'Mandy Claus' started that early."

She hesitated. But then again, she was chewing.

When she finished her bite, Mandy said, "I was exaggerating."

All Jake could see was her profile. She'd become deeply engrossed in watching the band tune up.

If past experience was any indication, she hadn't been exaggerating, any more than her ankle had been sprained on their first date.

# Chapter 9

Today was the day.

Or, more precisely, tonight.

Mandy put on her makeup with a shaky hand. The town hall meeting was at seven, and Jake would be speaking his piece. Her stomach had been doing flip-flops all day.

She'd still known Jake less than a month, but it had been the most unforgettable time of her life since that long-ago night when she was eight years old. A dizzying blend of the magic and the mundane, where simple things like having a cup of coffee or watching a movie at home turned into something special. A terrifying blend of pride and nerves as the people she'd known all her life saw her with Jake. And somehow, seemingly of one accord, kept their mouths shut. She wondered if her conversation with Sherry had played any part in that.

Tonight's meeting might determine if Jake would stay or if he would go.

Mandy closed her lipstick tube, shut her eyes and tried to form her thoughts into some kind of prayer. It would help if she knew what she was praying for.

For Jake to be happy.

For Jake to stay.

For Jake never to find out about Mandy's . . . nonconformity.

She couldn't keep it a secret if he stayed. It was amazing her luck had held out this long. It had never been a secret before.

She looked at the small wooden plaque above the bathroom mirror. It was one of her creations, and the only trace of Christmas in this little room. In alternating red and green letters, with a painted pattern that suggested a patchwork quilt, it simply read, BELIEVE.

She'd been denying a huge part of herself for too long.

Tomorrow, she told herself, she would buy those replacement frames for the clippings. Regardless of the outcome tonight.

Mandy closed her eyes and took a deep breath, the unformed prayer still in her head as she slowly exhaled.

\* \* \*

She'd planned to meet Jake at the town council chambers, but she was so keyed up she left the house ridiculously early. She looked at her watch and made the turn for Jake's hotel instead. The odds were he hadn't left yet, and he might appreciate the show of moral support.

Mandy white-knuckled the steering wheel, willing any mixed feelings out of her head.

When Jake opened the door of his room, he looked ready to go. More than ready. Breath whooshed out of Mandy's lungs.

He wore a navy pinstripe suit with a deep navy necktie. It made his brown eyes appear darker, determined.

In a word, he looked gorgeous.

To add another word—intimidating.

"Too much?" He glanced down. "It was this or the brown tweedy one."

"I'm not sure," Mandy stammered. "I've never been to a town council meeting."

"No reason you should. They're kind of like root canals." Jake straightened a tie that didn't need straightening. "You don't go in for one unless you really need to."

He stepped back from the door and eyed his reflection in the mirrored dresser at the foot of the bed. "I was thinking dress to impress," he said. "Now I'm thinking, maybe it's overkill."

He fiddled with the tie again. He couldn't seem to leave it alone, and that was so unlike Jake. It reminded her of the day he'd kept fidgeting with the cracker packets. Mandy walked up behind him and hugged his waist.

"Well, *you* seem to like it." Jake turned to clasp his arms around her. "What do you think? Wall Street power suit? Or the more laid-back one?"

She looked up at him. Snappy. Impressive. She didn't think anyone who didn't know Jake would guess how nervous he was.

"You look great," she said, and meant it.

Or was it too much for Tall Pine?

"Well, it's the one I started with. Guess I'd better not overthink it." Jake gave her a quick kiss. "Thanks for coming. It was a nice surprise." He picked up a leather portfolio from the top of the dresser. "Ready to go?"

Too late to change her mind now.

She nodded, her lungs empty of air for the second time.

When they reached the town hall, the meeting still wasn't due to start for fifteen minutes. Mandy's heels clacked on the hard, glossy floor of the lobby. Seeing a sign for the ladies' room, she gave Jake's arm a quick squeeze.

"Be right back," she said.

She ducked into the ladies' room, rushed to the stall farthest from the door, and threw up.

These places always reminded Jake of a courtroom. Maybe because the courthouse was always next door to city hall, probably built at the same time by the same contractor.

He and Mandy walked through the double glass doors of the town council chambers. Rows of chairs faced a raised stage with a long, desk-like panel, half a dozen seats behind it for the council members. None of the council chairs were occupied yet.

Usually, Jake didn't have to go through this step. In most of the cities he'd been to, the permit would have been issued at the counter where he'd started. He wondered if that would have been the case in Tall Pine if the project had been just another small independent business.

So far, only about a dozen of the public chairs were filled, and there wasn't another business suit in sight.

Jake led Mandy to a row of seats by the podium that also faced the seats of the council members. It stood roughly in the middle of the room. Most residents at the meeting would either have to turn around to see him, or if they were sitting behind him, look at the back of his head. The row they sat in would, at least, have a side view.

Taking her seat next to him, Mandy looked as queasy as he felt. Jake tried to keep his thoughts focused on the moment. One thing at a time. Right now the "one thing" was this meeting, and scoring as many points as possible. Get the project approved, and he could look forward to spending more time in Tall Pine.

Now wasn't the time to worry about why this project, and Tall Pine, mattered so much. He wouldn't want to be shot down on a project even if Tall Pine's sole population was a field full of gophers.

But it wasn't a field of gophers. Tall Pine had Mandy in it.

Just before seven, the council members filed in, four men and two women. He'd met them all at one time or another by now. Only one of the men wore a suit; the others wore lightweight dress shirts. The average age was mid-forties, roughly fifteen years older than Jake. The lone suit-wearer—Winston Frazier, he remembered—looked another twenty years older than that.

Jake shifted in his chair and, involuntarily, tugged at the knot in his tie. It was going to be a long meeting.

As it turned out, Jake's turn came up forty-five minutes later, after a discussion of rising water bills, quick approval for a new traffic light near the school, and the formation of a committee to explore the possibility of installing dispensers to sell duck feed at the lake.

"Next order of business." Rick Brewster, in one of the white button-down shirts, looked enviably crisp and cool. "Proposed application for permit to construct a Regal Hotel in Tall Pine."

And suddenly, it was high noon. Jake stood and crossed the few steps to the podium, convinced he'd left part of his stomach in the seat behind him. Heads in the audience turned his way, and Jake couldn't imagine why he'd been so concerned about being seen.

He tried to leave his doubts behind him in his chair, along with that missing part of his stomach. He also wished he'd thought to shrug out of his suit jacket while he had the chance, but it was too late now. He introduced himself and started speaking, feeling like a toboggan launching off the top of a snowy hill. No turning back.

"I'm aware that this project would be something of a precedent," he said, "and I'm aware of some of the possible objections to it. A lot of you may be concerned that a national chain like Regal Hotels would change the character of Tall Pine. This is a small mountain community, and that's the very nature of its charm. To date, all the businesses in Tall Pine are independent operations, and I applaud you for that. You've succeeded in maintaining a steady flow of tourist traffic."

Jake's eyes skimmed over the six council members. No visible reaction. It felt like talking to Mount Rushmore, with two extra faces.

He turned about forty-five degrees, spreading his gaze to include some of the public audience at his right. No visible reaction there either, but the room sure was quiet. And he was just now getting to the tough part.

"But sometimes *maintaining* business isn't enough. If Tall Pine doesn't make an effort to grow, you run the risk that more of those tourists will keep driving. Toward the next big thing. For a lot of them, that next thing is Mount Douglas. They have plenty of national chains. A ski resort. But a lot less of your charm.

"I'd like to suggest that a Regal Hotel would keep more visitors in Tall Pine. Our hotels are affordable, and one of the benefits of a national chain is consistency. People know what they're getting. It won't have the individual charm of your current independent hotels, but that's why I don't see Regal Hotels as a direct competitor to the two hotels already up here. Furthermore, if we located the Regal Hotel at one of the proposed sites—the old drive-in lot—we could offer people one more place to stop on their way farther up the mountain, and possibly get them to extend their stay in Tall Pine another day."

In the quiet room, he thought he heard Mandy exhale behind him. He hoped that meant he was doing well.

"You have a quiet community, and that's a great thing. But I don't think anyone would object to an increase in business. What I'm suggesting is that with carefully controlled growth, you can bring in more tourists without losing that personal touch. A Regal Hotel in Tall Pine would bring more tourist traffic to your shops and restaurants and help you share what your town has to offer."

Jake stopped. Time to let the ball bounce into their court. He fought the urge to fidget with his tie, holding on to the sides of the podium instead. "Questions?"

Once again, he tried to gauge the response from the six faces in front of him. He'd never seen such uniform neutrality. *You guys should play poker,* he thought.

"Well stated, Mr. Wyndham," Margery Williams said, and Jake could have kissed her for even moving. "But our concern has always been that once we allow one national chain, we can't very well say no to the others. How do you propose we control this growth?"

"That's up to you," Jake said. "I wouldn't want to stand in front of you and start dictating town policy. What I'm suggesting is that it's time for you to consider taking a small step. I'm sure that you could work out a policy that would carefully limit growth." He braced himself before he went on. "May I point out to you, you don't have any such policy now."

Frazier's scowl deepened; in the middle, Rick Brewster straightened.

Jake squared his shoulders. "Right now," he continued, "you don't have a code on the books against allowing a national chain in Tall Pine. The locations we're considering, like the old drive-in lot, are zoned for commercial use, and if it was a small, private hotel, I don't believe you'd have any objection."

Six faces, still expressionless, didn't argue.

*Careful.*

"A more aggressive business than Regal Hotels might ask for a more tangible legal argument for denying national franchises the right to pursue business here."

There wasn't a sound, but Jake could feel the tension rise in the room.

"I would *not* pursue any such action myself," Jake said slowly and clearly, "and speaking on behalf of Regal Hotels, I don't believe they would either. We're not interested in legal battles. Just in providing a profitable service and helping your community grow in the process. But without a

**129**

policy in place, you might be leaving yourselves open to problems with a more aggressive corporation in the future."

He didn't know if he'd neutralized the tension or not.

"If your answer is no," Jake said, "we'll move on. But what we'd rather do is stay here—and work with you to help Tall Pine grow." *Grow* was a scary word here. Jake amended, "To help your businesses prosper. And to share the charm of the community you've built so successfully."

"Thank you, Mr. Wyndham," Brewster said. He eyed the council members on his right, then on his left. "Is the council ready to put this to a vote?"

Suddenly they were shifting forward in their seats, and Jake's heart dropped into his shoes. A "yes" or "no" vote at this moment, with no time to deliberate, would almost certainly end in a "no." He needed a Plan B, and he'd better think fast.

"If I may," Jake began.

Was he really going to try to *delay* this?

If he had any hope of going forward, he'd better.

"If I were foolish enough to demand that you make a decision to change a long-standing town policy on the spot, I'm pretty sure I know how you'd vote," Jake said. "And I understand that. Major changes don't usually take place within ten minutes. Am I within my rights to suggest that you take some time to consider this before coming to a decision? Possibly form a committee?"

"You do seem to have a knack for making suggestions about town policy, Mr. Wyndham," Brewster said.

"Not my intention," Jake said. "I'm coming to you with a proposal. Not an ultimatum. What I'd like is to provide you all with some time to weigh both sides of the issue. The misgivings are easy to see. I'd like to allow you time to consider the possible benefits."

Brewster looked him up and down, and Jake's suit felt increasingly warm. Winston Frazier sat farther back from the panel.

"Does anyone second the motion to table this decision until the next town council meeting?" Brewster asked.

"I second," Margery Williams said.

The six-member town council voted three to two in favor of making a decision at the next meeting, with Rick Brewster abstaining. A committee was formed to evaluate the project, consisting of Brewster, Williams and Frazier. It felt like a stay of execution, but Jake thanked them and turned to rejoin Mandy. She looked paler than ever.

If he'd been running, he'd be bending forward and clutching his knees now. Too bad the pose was out of the question in a three-piece suit, in the town council chambers.

Jake settled beside Mandy and sat quietly through the rest of the meeting, taking pains to maintain his posture and appear to listen politely, although he had no idea what was being said. Something about a program to ensure that residents maintained their rain gutters.

Mandy slipped her hand into his on the arm of the seat between them. Her fingers, interlaced with his, felt cold. But somehow, her touch helped.

"Well, that could have gone better." Back at Jake's hotel room, he shrugged out of his suit jacket as if he were shedding an unwanted skin.

Mandy cringed inwardly. The drive back to the hotel had been a quiet one. But at least it was short. On the brief ride back, the one thing they established was that neither of them had eaten since lunch, so they'd stopped back at the hotel for Jake to change before they got a bite to eat.

"I thought you were great," Mandy said. "I was proud of you."

"Thanks." Jake hung the jacket in the room's shallow little closet, clearly anxious to be rid of it. "It wasn't exactly what they're wearing in Tall Pine this season, was it?"

"I'm sorry. I made the wrong call."

Jake pulled out a fresh shirt and slacks from

the closet. "Don't worry about it. How would you know?"

She winced. *I should have said something while I had the chance.*

Clothes over his arm, he started toward the bathroom to change. Then he turned back to her, his thick hair ruffled, navy tie askew.

"Did I ever say thank you?" he asked. "I mean, for being here tonight."

His eyes were aimed at her, but he still wore a distracted look. He didn't seem quite like Jake. Or maybe this was just a side of Jake she hadn't seen before—uncertain and off guard.

"You did." She mustered a smile. "Did I say you're welcome?"

"I have no idea," he admitted. He stepped back to Mandy and kissed her forehead. Her forehead? He was somewhere else, all right. "I'll go get changed. Be right back."

While she waited, Mandy eyed the side of the closet exposed by the sliding door Jake had left open. A small, practical assortment of polo shirts, one other dress shirt, a couple of pairs of slacks. He did travel light.

Packing would be easy.

She sighed and sat down heavily on the foot of the bed. She could see her reflection in the mirror above the dresser a few feet in front of her. She looked pale, and her light makeup job did little to disguise it.

She didn't know how much the suit, in and of itself, had hurt Jake's chances, but she'd give anything for another opportunity to change her answer. She didn't want him to go anywhere, and she couldn't imagine why there'd been any doubt in her mind. Maybe her thinking would have been clearer if she wasn't so preoccupied with hiding the truth about herself. Had her fear made her blurt out the wrong answer?

Enough was enough. She should have told him long before this. She'd tell him—

Jake emerged from the bathroom, looking much more like himself. A neat blue polo, crisp slacks, his hair and his smile both back in place. And killer brown eyes.

She'd tell him. Tomorrow.

"Ready to go?" he asked.

Mandy nodded. Jake took her hands and pulled her to her feet, so they stood close together in the small space between the bed and the dresser. Looking at him, she felt her eyes prickle. She blinked and glanced away, not quite fast enough. She felt him searching her face.

"Hey, are you okay?"

She studied the fibers on the shoulder of his shirt. "I just—" She sucked in a breath. "I feel like I let you down." She risked meeting his eyes, willing hers to stay dry. "And I really want you to stay."

It wouldn't make any sense to him, but she wanted to make sure he knew she meant it.

"What, are you still worried about the suit?" He squeezed her hands lightly. "That's the least of my problems. If they're going to be scared of a twenty-nine-year-old in pinstripes, that's because I didn't get them to see past it. My problem is making sure I get my point across. I ended up punting tonight, because I went in underprepared." He smiled ruefully. "I guess I've been a little distracted."

If he'd meant it as some kind of a compliment, it didn't have that effect. She averted her eyes again.

"Come on," he said. "Let's get some food before we faint."

She made herself smile. "You're on."

He kissed her again. On the cheek.

No, he definitely wasn't himself tonight.

# Chapter 10

Mandy only knew of one place that served the kind of drink she liked, so she directed Jake to the Foggy Notion, a busy little cafe on Evergreen Lane.

"*What* did you order?" Jake asked after the waiter took their drink orders and left them with their menus.

"It's called a Gingerbread Spritzer," she said. "It's got raspberry juice, ginger ale, cinnamon . . . There's no alcohol in it. And it really does taste a lot like a gingerbread man."

His brow furrowed. "Where'd you find out about a thing like that?"

"Here. It was a special on one of those little stand-up displays on the table." Mandy fingered the current placard next to the salt and pepper shakers. Tonight it was promoting their apple pie, which didn't sound like a bad idea either. "I don't think they invented it, but it's tasty."

"Leave it to you to find a drink that tastes like a Christmas cookie."

His smile might have been one of amusement or bewilderment, but Mandy decided it didn't matter either way. Anything to distract Jake seemed like a good idea at this point. From the time they left the hotel, he'd been analyzing what he'd done wrong and strategizing what to do next.

He was back at it now.

"I've been going about this all wrong," he said. "I thought playing softball was the way to go. I didn't want to come off like some kind of a lobbyist. But the soft-sell isn't working. I wasted too much time glad-handing without getting down to the real subject. Direct is always better." He passed a hand roughly through his hair. "I'm not sure what I thought was going to happen in there."

Mandy nodded. He'd been chasing around the same theme for a while now, and it wasn't doing him any good.

"Take a look at your menu," she said. "Before you start on your first ulcer."

That might have gotten his attention, but she couldn't tell for sure. He did look at his menu.

Mandy started to reread her menu, remembered she'd already decided what she wanted, and glanced past Jake to the waiting area by the front entrance.

Scotty Leroux was standing at the register, paying

the hostess for a large white box that probably contained either a cake or a pie.

Scotty Leroux, the class clown and former bane of her existence.

Scotty Leroux, Winston Frazier's nephew. And maybe, just maybe, a chance to help Jake—and make up for her own mistake.

Mandy stood before she could talk herself out of it. Jake looked up. His eyes still held that hazy, preoccupied look, and her heart wrenched a little. Tonight had been rough. It was almost as if they weren't sitting at the same table, and she missed him.

"Be right back," she said, resting a hand on Jake's shoulder as she sidled past him. "If the waiter comes back, I'll have the angel hair pasta with Alfredo sauce."

She wondered if he'd remember that.

Mandy caught up to Scotty as he was picking up his box to leave. "What's the occasion?"

He stopped in surprise. "Vicki's birthday is tomorrow. I was going to surprise her at work."

Vicki Martinez. She'd been a junior when they graduated. She hadn't realized Scotty was dating her. "Tell her happy birthday for me."

"Okay." Scotty cracked a smile. "So what's up with you and the suit?"

"He's not a suit." Mandy tamped down her indignation. "He's a really nice guy. So, you were at the council meeting?"

"Two rows back from you. I wanted to hear about the duck-feed thing."

Mandy craned her neck up a little. Scotty stood several inches taller than Jake, and Jake was far from short. "Scotty, I need a favor."

"You're kidding." He leaned against the counter where the hostess had rung up his pie, as if to say, *This has got to be good.* "What do you mean?"

"Could you talk to your uncle? Ask him to meet with Jake?"

"You *are* kidding. Why would he listen to me?"

"It's worth a try." She remembered Frazier's implacable expression. "Scotty, Jake really *is* a good guy. I just feel like the council had their minds made up before he ever went in there. If Winston would *listen* to him . . . then maybe the rest of them would, too."

"I don't know. He's a pretty stubborn old guy."

"And he's one-third of the committee." Mandy glanced across the room at Jake's back. He was starting to fidget with his menu. "Please, just ask. All I want is for Jake to have a fair chance."

Scotty contemplated her, then nodded. "Okay, I'll ask. But I can't promise anything."

Mandy cast her eyes around and found a pen in a jar on the counter. She scrawled Jake's number on the back of one of the restaurant's business cards and handed it to Scotty.

"Just try," she said. "Thanks."

"Okay." He took the card from her and pocketed it with a smile.

"You know, you're a pretty decent guy yourself," Mandy admitted.

"Of course."

"But I'm still not sure if it makes us even for 'Mandy Claus.'"

"Hey, a good line is a good line." Straightening from his lounging act against the counter, he adjusted his hold on the cake. "You know, you might not be dealing with all this if you'd gone out with me."

"But then Vicki might not be getting her cake tomorrow."

"True."

Plus, when he'd asked her out their senior year, after years of calling her Mandy Claus, she'd been half-convinced it was a joke. "You would have made fun of me anyway," she said.

"Well, sure." Scotty looked down at her with a lopsided grin. "When you're six feet tall before you hit junior high, you learn not to be too serious about anything."

While Mandy chewed on that, Scotty cuffed her shoulder lightly on his way out. "Good luck with the suit."

\* \* \*

Moments after Mandy left the table, the waiter brought their drinks. Jake tried to remember what she'd asked him to order and found he couldn't. Something about pasta.

"Thanks," Jake said as the server set the glasses down. "We'll be ready to order in a few minutes."

The waiter nodded and left.

Jake sighed. He'd been playing Monday morning quarterback, both out loud and in his head, ever since the town council meeting. He was starting to get sick of himself.

It brought back memories. *This* was the guy his other girlfriends had complained about. All except his last, another rep at Regal Hotels who was almost as work-obsessed as he was. He didn't think he liked this guy very much. But maybe this was the guy he had to be, if he wanted to pull off this project. He'd have to work smarter, use his time more effectively. And that probably meant spending less time enjoying himself.

He felt as if he'd been on vacation. A vacation where he came back feeling relaxed and refreshed, until he set foot in the office and realized what a mess he had waiting for him.

He hadn't set out to be different here. It had happened by degrees, he supposed, but it had happened fast. Starting around the time a certain blue-eyed brunette had stepped from behind an artificial tree.

Where *was* Mandy, anyway?

He looked over his shoulder in the direction she'd gone. He'd figured the ladies' room.

Instead, she stood in the front waiting area, talking to the lanky Scotty Leroux.

The Neanderthal section of his brain felt an immediate surge of jealousy. Fortunately, the analytical side had the sense to step back and watch. He knew a little about body language, and what he saw didn't look much like a romantic tête-à-tête. She stood slightly back from Leroux, her posture taut, while he leaned against the counter, looking slightly amused.

Not romantic, at least not at the moment, but he got the impression there was some kind of history there. All because of that nickname? Really?

Then Leroux started out of the lobby, giving her shoulder a pat as he went, and she smiled. Jake hadn't gotten many smiles out of her tonight. He had himself to blame for that, and that realization didn't help at all.

He should know better than to read too much into things, but the little scene grated on him like a rock in his shoe as Mandy returned to the table.

He couldn't stop himself. "So, did Scotty finally give you his class ring?"

It sounded more snide than he'd intended.

Mandy's face went through a quick series of reactions. First, she looked as if she'd been caught. Then, almost as if she'd been slapped.

Then, as if she'd really, really like to slap him back.

She didn't dignify the crack with a response. Instead she sat down, her eyes quietly taking in the fact that their drinks had arrived and their menus were still there. She didn't comment on that either. She picked up her tall red drink and sipped it.

Jake toyed with his coffee, thinking he probably should have ordered decaf. Not that he'd sleep much tonight anyway.

She reached for her glass again, but this time she slid it toward him. "Try it?"

It was as good a peace offering as any, and at least one of them was adult enough to do it. Jake didn't find the tall red concoction particularly tempting, but he picked it up and took a sip. Not bad, actually.

"You're right," he said. "It does taste like gingerbread."

He set the glass down in front of Mandy. Then, resting his hand on the table, he laid his fingers lightly over hers. She met his eyes with what was almost a smile.

Jake felt it again, like a faint hum running up his arm—that funny little current that seemed to connect them, like a battery sliding into place.

"It's been a rough night," he said. "You've been awfully patient."

*I'm sorry for being a jerk* would have been more on the nose. But for some reason he couldn't make himself say it. So he went on for the rest of the evening, trying to apologize without actually apologizing, trying to stay away from shoptalk. The trouble was, that didn't leave much room for conversation, since that was all that kept swirling through his mind.

He'd have to report to the home office in the morning, and he didn't know how that would turn out. Since he hadn't gotten a go-ahead from the town council, justifying another month up here to corporate wouldn't be easy. Just another area where he hadn't worked up a good Plan B. In all of tonight's rambling, that was one problem he'd managed to refrain from mentioning to Mandy. He didn't want to lay that on her, on top of everything else.

It was the first time he could remember having a hard time finding something to say to her.

After dinner, he drove Mandy back to the hotel and walked her to her car.

"It feels weird leaving you here," he said. "I should be dropping you off at home."

She quirked a little smile at him. "I'm pretty sure I can find my way."

Standing under the parking lot's weak streetlamp, she looked tired. And beautiful. Jake framed her face in his hands and did what he should have done hours ago.

He kissed her, not a quick peck the way he'd done earlier tonight, but the way he always did. He could tell the awkward evening had taken a toll on Mandy, because at first she didn't respond the way she usually did. He didn't blame her. But he didn't give up so easily. He folded his arms around her gently, bringing one hand up to tunnel his fingers through her long, smooth hair. Soon her arms were around him, too, and it was a long time before either of them let go.

He hadn't said anything right all night.

This was better.

Finally he rested his cheek on top of her head and just held her. Mandy sighed, and he hoped that meant they were back where they'd been when the evening started. Where they should be.

Mandy spoke against his chest. "Jake?"

"Hmm?"

"What happens next?"

"Well, unfortunately, I guess you drive home without me."

"You know what I mean."

Of course he did. He'd just been hoping, all night, that she wouldn't ask.

"I talk to corporate in the morning." With Mandy in his arms, the words felt foreign. He felt like his more recent, Tall Pine self. *I'd much rather be this guy.*

"And?"

"And, don't borrow trouble. It's too late at night for 'what-ifs.' I'll find out tomorrow."

It was the kind of thinking that had landed him in this predicament to begin with. But strategizing at this hour wouldn't do him any good. He needed sleep first, and a little perspective.

So he kissed her again. It might be the cheapest way to avoid any more questions, but it was also the most worthwhile.

Having Mandy in his arms, he decided, didn't feel like being on vacation.

It felt like home.

# Chapter 11

The ugly, ugly ringing of Jake's cell phone sounded next to his bed. He felt as if he'd been hit by an especially ill-tempered truck.

But as he reached for the phone, he didn't feel the disorientation that came from being wakened from a sound sleep. It had been a restless night, and he was well aware of where he was and what was happening. Nevertheless, the time displayed on the screen of the phone astonished him: six-ten in the morning.

Yes, Scranton was three hours ahead. But the corporate office should realize California was three hours behind.

"Good morning," Jake answered dryly.

It was Mark, his regional director. "How'd the meeting go? I didn't hear from you last night."

"That's because I knew it was midnight your time," Jake said pointedly.

Of course, in the past, he probably would have texted or e-mailed. He really *had* been obsessive.

He should have let his phone go to voice mail to give himself time to wake up and gather his thoughts. That ship had sailed. So he propped himself up on the pillows, making himself at least semi-vertical, and told Mark about the meeting as neutrally as he could.

"Do you think this one's worth pursuing?" Mark asked.

Jake tried, with all his resolve, to be objective. It had never come to this. Normally, setbacks and delays were only red tape, not outright resistance. Would he still want to chase Tall Pine if Mandy weren't here? Yes, he decided. Because he wouldn't want to lose. But maybe that wasn't a good enough reason.

Instead, he reminded Mark of the assets that had drawn them to Tall Pine in the first place. A quiet, scenic location less than two hours from Los Angeles. An untapped market. A reasonable tourist trade of people wanting a weekend getaway.

It all still made sense on paper. Until you added in the other column, with the six faces of the town council on the other side.

Margery Williams had been fairly empathetic. Winston Frazier, silently antagonistic. Jake had probably alienated Rick Brewster, and the other three were an unknown quantity.

But those unknowns had voted in favor of a committee.

"Can you make it fly?" Mark persisted.

*What happens if I don't?* Jake's job might not be on the line, but his track record was. A perfect track record. He could walk away and leave it intact.

"Yes," he said. "I think I can make it work."

If Mark noticed the wording, *I think,* he didn't acknowledge it.

Instead, Mark asked, "The next town council meeting isn't until next month?"

Mandy sat on the sofa to put on her shoes, trying to put on her resolve at the same time. Today, she was going to tell Jake.

Her cell phone rang.

"Mandy?" Jake's voice sounded far away and distorted.

"Jake? I'm having trouble hearing you."

"Sorry. I'm using the Bluetooth. I'm on my way to the airport."

Her heart lurched.

"They called me back in to the home office. I'll be gone a couple of weeks."

Mandy remembered Jake's spartan hotel room with the orderly, nearly empty closet. That closet must be empty now.

"We touched base about the meeting last night,

**149**

and they want me back to catch up on things at the office."

She gulped. That couldn't be good. It didn't help that the phone connection made him sound so far away.

"Mandy? Are you there?"

She found herself talking louder, trying to cover the distance. "I'm here." *But you're not.*

"I know the timing's awful. It wasn't my idea. I'll be back. And I'll call you while I'm gone."

She gripped the phone, wishing the connection between them didn't feel so tenuous. Her free hand clutched the stomach that hadn't recovered yet from yesterday.

In a way, it was a reprieve. She'd resolved to tell him the truth; surely, over the telephone, the truth could wait. She'd have time to think about what to say. To stall.

To worry about it.

This could be a good thing, Jake tried to tell himself.

A couple of weeks away would give him a chance to think more objectively and weigh his priorities. Because they'd certainly changed in the short month he'd spent in Tall Pine. Maybe, back at the office, he'd be able to concentrate, work smarter, and figure out what he'd been doing wrong.

He tried to play the town hall meeting over in his head like a transcript. Heaven knew the words were emblazoned in his memory. But what he kept hearing was Mandy's voice on the other end of the cell phone connection.

And he kept feeling, even as he drove to the airport and boarded the eastbound flight, that he was heading in the wrong direction.

During the two-hour layover in Dallas, his phone rang.

It was Winston Frazier.

"Mr. Wyndham, I'll be honest. I didn't think this Regal Hotel proposal would make it past last night."

*Well, thanks for your honesty.*

"Now with this committee, it doesn't look like it's going to go away." Frazier cleared his throat. "My nephew suggested you and I meet to talk about it."

Jake frowned. "Your nephew?"

"Scott Leroux."

A *click* sounded in Jake's brain as the puzzle piece snapped into place. He saw Mandy standing in the restaurant last night in that semirigid stance and remembered Leroux's amused look. Jake had given her a hard time for talking to the guy.

"I'd be glad to meet with you," Jake said. "There's only one problem. . . ."

And he had the pleasure of telling Frazier he was on his way across the country. If the old man

**151**

hadn't sounded thrilled before, he sounded less thrilled now. Why couldn't Mark have waited a few more days to bring him in?

Still, it was a foot in the door, and Jake would keep that foot wedged there even if it meant stretching his leg three thousand miles across the United States.

"Mr. Frazier, I'll call you to set this up, as soon as I'm able to check my schedule at the office. Will tomorrow morning work for you?"

"It'll do." Jake could have sworn he heard a grimace on the other end.

"Sir, I appreciate this. I know this wasn't anything you'd planned on, but I—" Jake cut himself off before he started trying to argue his case again. "I'm looking forward to hearing your thoughts."

That got a better reaction. "Yes. Well, I'll talk to you tomorrow."

Jake hung up. *Remember that. When you meet with him, don't just talk. Listen.*

That was Common Business Sense 101, and he hadn't been using it last night. Maybe his head was already starting to clear.

The thought didn't stop him from dialing Mandy's cell number immediately. It went to voice mail. Of course—she'd be at work. Jake checked his watch and saw he'd probably just missed her lunch break.

He hung up. He didn't want to use a recording to thank her, or a text message. But he didn't want to wait hours, either.

Jake gazed at the wallpaper image on his phone: a picture of Mandy, smiling, with the sunset lake behind her. He grinned.

*There's an app for that,* he thought.

"Merry Christmas." Mandy handed her customer a bag containing a ceramic jack-o'-lantern. Both of them laughed at the mixed message.

Mrs. Swanson had left after lunch, so Mandy had the store to herself. She beamed at every customer who walked in, and she didn't have to fake the smile. Every new person who came through the door brought a welcome opportunity to keep busy. She put a Bing Crosby CD on the store sound system and let the old favorites wash over her. It almost helped, except it reminded her that "White Christmas" had been playing the first time Jake came into The North Pole.

He had said he'd be back. She needed to believe that and not worry. The trick was to stay occupied in the meantime.

Mandy eyed the fall display table and thought of something she could work on.

Across from the pumpkins, she started a display

of Christmas crafts: needlepoint kits for stockings, embroidery kits for pillows, figurines and ornaments to paint. She made a mental note to set them out earlier next year. She'd meant to do it before Jake arrived, but—to use Jake's word—she'd gotten distracted.

She was close enough to the counter to hear her cell phone when it rang in her purse. The muffled electronic chime of "Deck the Halls" struggled to compete with Bing Crosby.

Mandy circled the counter to check the phone. It had gone to voice mail by the time she picked it up. The call log displayed Jake's number.

Before she could check for a message or try to call back, a woman walked in with three little girls. Quickly, Mandy stashed her phone.

The girls went straight to the craft-table-in-progress, and soon Mandy was busy helping their mother find projects to suit their ages. While she talked with her customers, Mandy heard the sound of jingling bells from behind the counter—the tone that signaled she'd gotten a text.

When her customers left, Mandy beelined to the counter to open the message. It took several seconds to load.

Then a snow globe materialized on her screen, tiny white flakes falling inside, with an animated

Santa Claus soaring upward in a reindeer-drawn sleigh.

Instead of a Christmas greeting, there were two lines of text in a festive cursive font: *Winston called. THANK YOU.*

And below, in smaller letters: P.S. Please excuse the corny St. Nick.

Mandy felt a warm flush from her head to her feet.

Maybe Jake understood her better than she thought.

At first Jake told himself it was jet lag.

Pennsylvania felt different from what he remembered. The walls of the office felt closer, more confining. His desk had managed to pick up a fine layer of dust. Even his own apartment felt impersonal, out of use, not much more homey than his hotel room in Tall Pine.

He'd arrived back in town just in time for a series of first-quarter planning meetings, one of the major reasons Mark had wanted him back. The meetings themselves were death, but getting ready for them required the kind of financial projections Jake usually loved sinking his teeth into. Now he found himself restless, bored, distracted.

*Still* distracted?

He made an appointment with Winston Frazier for the second week in October, and he counted that as his most tangible accomplishment so far.

A few days after he arrived, he ran into Lorraine at the copy machine. They'd been smiling and nodding at each other in the hallway for days, but this was the first time he found himself face-to-face with her long enough to call for any sort of conversation.

Awkward. They'd broken up six months ago, after a year and a half of dating. Since then they hadn't spent enough time in the same city to establish any kind of a new "normal."

But Lorraine, one of those tall women who wasn't timid about wearing heels, was all smiles as she picked up her copies. She stepped back to make room for him at the machine. "So, how was California?"

"Complicated." Jake laid a spreadsheet on the copier.

"No swimming pools, movie stars?"

"Nope." Jake hit the button. "Pine trees, mountain cabins."

"Sounds more like here."

"Not exactly." He grinned, remembering his first conversation with Mandy. "Out there, snow is something they drive up to visit."

"So, what got complicated?"

"A cranky town council that meets once a month. It's a long story."

"Want to talk about it at lunch?"

Jake hesitated. A simple thing like lunch shouldn't be a landmine for misinterpretation. Their breakup had been mutual, or so he'd thought.

He met her eyes. "Burgers, Dutch?" That should be clear enough.

Lorraine's smile didn't falter. "Sure."

He knew he was taking a chance. But Lorraine was a bright woman, she'd always been a good sounding board, and they ought to establish that new normal at some point.

They ate at a hamburger chain, the kind of place Tall Pine wouldn't abide. Jake explained the town's unwritten policy while they waited at the table for their numbers to be called. Numbers, not names. Once again, Jake had a sense of culture shock.

"The thing is, they have a point," he said. "Part of the appeal of Tall Pine is that it's away from all this stuff."

"Stuff?"

"Franchises. Corporate America. If a chain hotel comes in, they're afraid it could lead to a lot more." He felt like a broken record, except that Lorraine hadn't heard it yet.

Their orders came up. As they ate, Jake realized it wasn't awkward at all. It was familiar. Very much

**157**

the same way they'd interacted when they were dating.

Then again, that had been part of the problem. They'd called it off, in large part, because they felt like colleagues more than anything else. So, did this feel like a date or not? Being with her reminded him simultaneously of why they'd gone out for a year and a half, and why they'd broken up.

As Lorraine started talking about possible strategies, it was like listening to himself. Shoptalk. No flights of fancy or quirky conversations about ghosts and what Santa Claus should look like. With Mandy, there was always something more to talk about—except for that final night, when he'd been letting the town council meeting eat him alive.

"So, is it worth it?" Lorraine asked. She'd come back around to Mark's question.

"For Regal Hotels, I'm not sure," Jake confessed. "Maybe we're better off sticking to the cities and suburbs. But for me—I just can't let it go."

He could tell her about quiet lakes with ducks and geese, or thin mountain air that fought back against his lungs on his morning jog, or little shops and restaurants where at least two-thirds of the people knew Mandy by name. But that wasn't what he'd fallen in love with.

He hoped Lorraine wouldn't curse him for a

jerk. But he looked her in the eye and told her what he should have made clear at the beginning.

"I met someone there," he said.

Intelligent gray eyes studied him. "And . . . it's complicated?"

He thought about Mandy—her sparkle, her openness, her strange contradictions. "Complicated" was one word for it, but . . .

He shook his head. "She's amazing."


"I usually stick with the reds and greens," Mandy admitted. "But I'm pretty traditional. There's nothing wrong with thinking outside the box."

Across the table from her, Renee was fast finishing the first project of The North Pole's new Tuesday-night Christmas craft class: a hand-painted wooden ornament. Mandy had started with the simplest project she could think of, something that would be easy for someone of any skill level to complete and take home. She'd been especially pleased when Renee, the mother of the two girls she'd met with Jake, had shown up.

Now the four other women in the class peered over the table with murmurs of admiration at Renee's Christmas stocking, painted in purples and golds, with striking results.

"I had to use purple," Renee said. "It's Bailey's favorite color."

Mandy glanced at the clock. "You've got time for at least one more. Maybe two."

In the center of the table, along with the paints, Mandy had laid out a selection of precut shapes in neat stacks: candy canes, Christmas trees, stockings, gingerbread men.

Renee reached for another stocking. "This one's for Rosie. It's going to be worse."

"Pink?" Mandy and the other women said in unison.

Renee grinned and nodded. "I think every little girl goes through the pink stage."

Mandy wondered if Emily, the niece Jake talked about, liked pink.

She glanced at the clock again and tried to calculate how long she'd gone without thinking about Jake. He'd been gone a week, and he called her regularly, but their quick catch-up phone conversations were no substitute for his presence.

The craft class had been a good idea, one she should have thought of years ago. It was a perfect way to bring people into the store during the off-season. Still, her reason for starting the class had been entirely selfish. It gave her one more way to stay busy.

Debra looked over the assortment of shapes on the cookie sheet and reached for a gingerbread man. "I'm surprised," she said. "You don't have any Santa Clauses."

Mandy decided to skip her *it's-so-hard-to-get-Santa-right* spiel. Debra had known her in elementary school. She knew all about Mandy and Santa.

"You're right," Mandy said. "I'll have to remember that next time."

Debra persisted. "Do you still believe in Santa Claus?"

Mandy didn't hesitate. "Sure," she said. "Doesn't everyone?"

It had become her standard answer, and people usually didn't have a follow-up question. Mandy brushed some darker green shading onto the Christmas tree ornament she'd been painting.

"Bailey told me your story about seeing Santa Claus," Renee said. "She loved it."

Mandy kept concentrating on her work, aware of a few more eyes on her. Renee was the only person at the table who hadn't grown up here.

Tish asked, "Did you ever stop believing it?"

Five heads turned expectantly in Mandy's direction, Renee's expression more curious than the rest.

Mandy did what she'd learned to do way back in grade school. She played it light.

"Three things I never argue about," she said. "Religion, politics, and Santa Claus."

"You mean it really happened?" Renee asked.

All five of them waited.

"I saw him," Mandy said cheerfully. "Plain as day."

Five faces, including Renee's, looked at her with varying degrees of puzzlement. Then they all got back to work.

This was the way it had been for years. People gawked a little, sometimes teased her, and life went on. This wasn't elementary school anymore. The ground didn't open up; it was a fact of life. She'd have to remember that when she talked to Jake.

But, nice as the women were, their reaction didn't matter nearly so much.

# Chapter 12

Mandy carefully aligned the second newspaper clipping in its frame, eyeing it from the front before she turned it over to fit the backing into place.

She'd bought the frames weeks ago—one red and one green. She'd kept them quietly stashed away so Mrs. Swanson wouldn't bring them up. October was half over, but Mrs. Swanson had given her until the beginning of November. Now Mandy stashed them one more time, far back on the shelf under the counter. Putting the clippings in their frames was one more step.

The last step would be to hang them. After she talked to Jake.

He'd be back tonight. The thought set a jumble of emotions tumbling through her like clothes in a dryer. Excitement. Apprehension. Uncertainty. On the phone, he'd given her updates on his progress, frustrations and setbacks at the Scranton office.

She'd filled him in on the craft classes and the cold nights they'd been having up here lately. Now they'd been apart almost as long as they'd been together, and she wondered if they'd have to get to know each other all over again.

The last week had been the hardest. His supervisor had kept him an extra week; apparently Jake was the only person fit to present the next quarter's projections to the corporate higher-ups. He'd had to reschedule his meeting with Winston Frazier, and Jake hadn't sounded happy about it.

The front door bells jingled, and two women drifted in. One was Renee; the other, with matching dark blond hair, had to be her sister.

"Hi," Renee said. "This is my sister, Brenda. We wanted to pick up a couple of your needlepoint pillow kits."

"Great." Mandy came around to the craft table. "We've got three over here. They're the most popular ones. Then we've got some more in that row near the back."

Brenda said, "Do you have any with cats?"

Mandy grinned and pointed again toward the back. Business was definitely picking up. The chillier the nights and the shorter the days, the more people seemed to find their way into the Christmas store. Next week they'd start interviewing temporary part-time employees for the holiday season.

As the two women moved away, the phone rang.

"Welcome to The North Pole," Mandy said into the phone.

The now-familiar filtered sound of a cell phone connection reached her ear. "Mandy?"

*Not another delay.* "Hi, Jake."

"Would you be able to go on a break in twenty minutes or so?"

Her heart jumped. "Why?"

"Because I'm about nineteen minutes away. And . . ." The phone went quiet, and Mandy thought they might have lost the connection. "I miss you."

Mandy glanced over her shoulder at the two sisters huddled in the craft aisle. "Mrs. Swanson's gone for the day, so I can't go anywhere, but . . ." She felt a smile spread over her face. "Come on in."

Renee and Brenda came up a few minutes later, each with a pillow kit. Mandy chuckled as she rang them up: one with a puppy design, one with a kitten. "Cats and dogs?" she asked.

"We fought like cats and dogs when we were kids," Brenda said.

Mandy eyed the clock as she made small talk and learned that Brenda was visiting from San Diego. At last Mandy sent them on their way with a "Merry Christmas" and three minutes to spare.

Two minutes later, Jake was in the store.

As he made his way toward her, Mandy had time to take in that he'd had a haircut; that his eyes were a deeper brown than she remembered; that he had a five o'clock shadow and his shirt looked slightly rumpled, as if he'd been traveling since early this morning.

By the time Mandy made her way from behind the counter, he'd reached her.

He took her in his arms, and it was almost a collision. Mandy held on tight, feeling his lips on her face and in her hair. He felt so warm and solid, so *real,* Mandy couldn't believe he'd felt so far away all this time.

"Sorry," he murmured against her hair. "I've been dying to do this for hours. Weeks."

Mandy glanced over his shoulder at the door, wondering if she would have heard the store bells if anyone walked in. Seeing no one, she pulled him behind the Christmas tree at the end of the nearest aisle. He kissed her, long and full, then held her so tightly she felt completely, blissfully engulfed. She could feel a heartbeat between them, but she couldn't tell if it was hers or his, or whether they'd synced up perfectly.

Resting a cheek on the front of his shirt, Mandy felt a giggle well up in her throat. "Welcome back."

*I think we just got reacquainted.*

His voice muffled in the hair that fell alongside her neck, he murmured, "I hate Scranton."

A little out of breath, she asked, "Why?"

"Because you're not in it."

\* \* \*

She smelled wonderful, that indefinable combination of whatever soap and shampoo she used, along with the faint hint of cinnamon. Jake breathed her in and savored the feel of her small build in his arms. Slowly, he raised his head and reluctantly started to disentangle himself, self-conscious now about his bull-in-a-china-shop version of a reunion.

"I haven't checked into my hotel yet. And I'd better let you get back to work." He kissed the top of her head, not moving any farther just yet. "Sorry for stomping in like this. It's been a long three weeks."

"Don't apologize." Her arms squeezed around his waist.

He cupped her face in his hands and drank in the sight of her blue eyes, like deep, refreshing pools. "I'll go get checked in and cleaned up," he said. "Can I pick you up here at five?"

She nodded.

Jake stepped out the door of the store, hearing the jingle of its bells, feeling the fresh slap of the mountain air. It might be colder here than in Scranton, he realized. The weeks he'd been gone had brought a marked shift in temperature up

**167**

here. This might be Southern California, but it felt downright wintry.

He climbed into the truck—not the same one he'd rented last time, but close enough—and drove the two-and-a-half minutes to the same hotel. As Phyllis checked him in, he couldn't tell if she was happy to see him again or not, but he'd worry about that tomorrow.

The last two hours before the store closed dragged by, in spite of the sales of several of the fall items, a pinecone necklace and a reindeer cookie jar.

From time to time Mandy glanced under the counter where the two framed clippings waited, safely enclosed in their shopping bags. She could hang them now, and there'd be less chance of losing her resolve.

But she still felt two inches off the ground just from being back in Jake's arms. What could one more night hurt?

At four-thirty, a couple came in with an adorable little boy somewhere around six years old. Mandy smiled at the mother as she guided her son cautiously past the shiny glass bric-a-brac. Definitely weekend visitors. It was Saturday, and they were in no hurry. Murphy's Law. You could always count on last-minute customers when you were hoping to get out of the store early. Mandy knew she wouldn't get a head start on closing the register tonight.

Mandy stayed at her post behind the counter and listened to the soft hum of chatter as the family drifted from one shelf to another. By the time they brought their son to the register with a Christmas stocking, it was nearly five.

The bells on the door jingled, and Jake walked in.

Mandy smiled past her customers at him, then rang up the stocking. She looked down at the little boy. "Are you going to hang this up over the fireplace this year?"

He nodded, his wide dark eyes adorably serious under straight black bangs.

Mandy bagged the purchase and handed it to Dad as he put his wallet away. He passed the bag to his son, who looked up at him questioningly.

"Go ahead," he said. "Ask her."

A frosty thrill crept down the back of Mandy's neck. She knew exactly where this was headed. She met the little boy's eyes and waited.

"Are you the lady who saw Santa Claus?" His voice was low and shy.

Mandy's eyes darted from the boy to Jake, who glanced up from the pumpkins at the fall display.

She'd never turned a child away in her life.

"That's me." Mandy came around the counter and did what she'd always done. Resting her hands on her knees, she brought herself closer to the boy's level, meeting those wide dark eyes. "Want me to tell you how it happened?"

A somber nod. Mandy's mouth felt dry. She was aware of the boy's parents, aware of Jake in the background, but when this moment came there was only one audience that mattered. As she started to speak, the words flowed out of her.

"Well, it was the night before Christmas, and I was eight years old," she began. "I stayed up late, and I was in my living room all by myself. Not a creature was stirring. Not even a mouse. . . ."

Jake stood a few feet away and watched Mandy weave magic.

It was time for the store to close, but he knew she wouldn't have told the family that for love or money. She spoke to the little boy in earnest, hushed tones—the perfect storytelling voice—and Jake heard every word. Even from where he stood, it was easy to forget that he was standing in the middle of a store on a late afternoon in October.

Her account built to a dazzling finish, with Santa vanishing up the chimney in a flash of light. For a moment everyone was silent.

"Did your mommy and daddy believe you?" the boy asked.

Something flickered in Mandy's eyes. "My mommy did," she said. "My daddy wasn't home."

"Were there reindeer on the roof?"

Mandy appeared to consider. "I didn't hear any prancing and pawing," she said. "But I think flying reindeer might be very quiet."

When no other questions came, Mandy straightened slowly and reached into the bowl on the counter. "Would you like a candy cane?" she offered. She smiled at the parents. "For after dinner, that is."

The three of them nodded. Mandy bent again to hand the boy the wrapped candy cane. "Merry Christmas," she said softly.

The little boy's eyes shone, and Jake felt like the witness to a timeless ritual. He watched the family file out, accompanied by the light jingling of the sleigh bells on the door. He turned to Mandy, whose gaze followed her visitors as they passed the store windows outside.

He was afraid to say anything that might break the spell, but Mandy beat him to it. As soon as the family was out of sight, she crossed to the front of the shop, turned the "Closed" sign around and locked the door.

"I'll need to close the register before we leave," she said. "It'll take a little extra time. Sorry."

Her tone was bright, almost brisk, as she pulled the drawer out of the cash register and slipped into the back room.

* * *

As Jake walked her outside the store, the cold air had a particularly sharp bite to it, and Mandy let herself huddle closer against his arm. She hadn't met his eyes since the family left. She knew he'd been listening, and she knew what was coming next.

She'd put off facing this for too long already, and she didn't think she was going to get the *one-more-night* she'd been promising herself.

When Jake climbed into the driver's seat, he turned to her before he started the car. "That was the sweetest thing I've ever heard."

She met his eyes and saw a faint echo of what she saw in the faces of the kids when she told them her story. He almost got it, she thought. If he could just be different from everyone else . . .

The trouble was, he was twenty years too old.

Mandy bit her lip. This was it. Before they'd even had dinner. If she didn't say it now, she never would, and he'd hear it from someone else.

"It isn't just a story," she said.

She waited, breathing slowly, for the look on his face she'd never wanted to see.

Jake's reaction was just what she'd always imagined.

She watched his smile fade as his expression shifted from a hesitant, *You're-kidding-right?* to a shell-shocked, *Oh-my-God-you're-serious.*

Her stomach clenched.

"Wait a minute," Jake said. "You don't really mean . . ."

"I saw Santa Claus," she said, summoning up her last shred of calm.

"You mean—like a dream, right? You said you fell asleep on the couch. . . ."

"No. I pinched myself. Hard. I still had a red mark the next day."

For the first time since grade school, she was actually trying to get someone to believe her. She'd given up arguing long ago. At least Jake wasn't making fun of her.

This was worse.

He closed his eyes, as if trying to concentrate. "Okay. Let's break this down."

*No. No. No.* She didn't need the practical, logical Jake. She needed the playful, monster-movie-loving Jake.

Why should he be different from anyone else?

*Because I need him to be.*

He looked at her as if he'd just come up with an original argument. "If it was really Santa Claus, why didn't he give you a present?"

"It's not like that." Her heart was going like a jackhammer. Discussion and logic had never done any good before, but for Jake, she'd try. "I'm not saying he goes around from house to house, handing out presents to everyone. It's like what my mother told me once: Santa Claus is the spirit of

**173**

Christmas. I don't understand all of it, or why it doesn't happen to more people. I think maybe sometimes if someone really believes in him—or really needs to see him—"

"You *needed* to see him." Jake nodded vigorously. "That's it. Don't you see? It was a rough year for you and your mom. It was the year your dad left. You waited on the couch to watch for Santa Claus, and you were probably half asleep—"

Mandy shook her head. Not vigorously. Slowly, with conviction. It was all she really had.

"You really believe it," he said.

Her shake of the head turned into a nod.

"I know what I saw," she said.

Jake studied her, his eyes quiet and serious. He lifted a hand to her cheek, and Mandy held perfectly still. She didn't know what she was hoping for. But the affection in Jake's eyes looked so honest, so undisguised—

He said, "I guess if it's gotten you through, it can't be all bad."

*Not* what she needed to hear. Mandy's heart fell with a thud.

Before she knew what she was doing, she was out of the truck, back in the cold air. Her eyes burned, and her mind had room for only two words.

*Get away. Get away.*

Of course it couldn't be that easy.

In an instant Jake was on the sidewalk in front of

her, his hands on her shoulders. He looked blurry, because God forbid, she felt her eyes brimming with tears.

*Get away. Don't let him see you like this.*

She tried to pull back, to escape back into the shop, but firm hands held her in place. His voice cut through. She didn't know if he'd spoken before or not.

"Mandy, *wait.*"

Her heart was past pounding now. She was sure it was going to burst out and land on the sidewalk between them. She swallowed hard, twice, remembering that she'd heard somewhere that it could keep you from crying. And suddenly, she had words again. They rushed out of her mouth.

"Jake, I've been through this since I was a kid. People humor me. I get it. But they're people I've known all my life. They know me, even if they think I'm a nut. 'Nice girl. Too bad she's a fruitcake.' If you'll pardon the expression. But *you*—"

Out of air, she sucked in a deep breath. She tried to turn away again, but Jake held on.

"Okay," he said. "I said the wrong thing. But you caught me off guard. Can you cut me a little slack? I never saw this coming. You're not giving me any time to process this."

Jake's mind struggled to catch up. This morning he'd been in Pennsylvania. Half an hour ago he'd been ecstatic just to be here. Now everything felt unreal, as if someone had told him the sun was going to set in the east tonight instead of the west. Except it felt like it might not have to set at all. The late afternoon was prematurely gray, bitter cold and devoid of color, except for Mandy's bright red jacket and deep blue eyes, glistening with tears she wouldn't let fall.

He wanted to hold her, to backtrack just ten or fifteen minutes, to put everything on pause until he could figure out how to fix this.

Mandy was waiting for him, and he was scrabbling for words that would turn this around instead of digging him deeper. He had nothing.

Mandy stepped back, her shoulders slipping from his grasp.

"Jake, I can take it from everyone else. 'Mandy Claus.' I've been hearing it since I was nine. I can live with it because I know what I saw. But from you . . ."

Her breath came out in clouds in front of her, as if she were winded.

"I hoped . . . I hoped you'd be different."

Her words died away, and the tears brimmed huge. "But *that's* crazy." Her voice was a ragged whisper as she turned away.

The words wrenched his heart. Jake caught her by the elbow.

"Wait," he said. That futile, useless word again. "Where are you going?"

"Home. My car is parked in back." She kept her face turned away.

He flailed for time. "It's cold. At least let me take you to it."

"I can cut through the store."

Her arm slipped again from his grasp, and she walked away, unlocking the store. Jake tried to think of a way to stop her, but every word he'd said so far had only made things worse. He couldn't come up with anything new. The word that kept coming back to him, uselessly, was *wait*.

But he didn't know what came after that. He needed to think, to sort this out, to regroup.

As Mandy closed the shop door behind her, Jake climbed back into the truck. He rounded the block to the exit of the alley in time to see Mandy's little red car back out safely and head toward the side street up into the hills that would take her home.

He wanted to follow her, to make sure she got there all right. But that probably bordered on creepy stalker behavior. In her current state of mind, he didn't think she'd appreciate it.

So, Jake turned up the heat in the truck and drove off through the premature gray.

# Chapter 13

When she got home, Mandy gave in and cried like the child she'd once been.

She didn't cry often, unless you counted movies. It felt as if she'd been saving this one up ever since she met Jake. She'd spent so much time wondering what would happen when this moment finally came. She thought she'd prepared herself for the worst. But deep down, all along, she'd hoped for better.

So she curled in a ball at the far end of the sofa and sobbed into a handy red cushion, wishing she'd remembered to grab a box of tissues first.

After ten or fifteen minutes, the cry-fest lost some of its steam. She slumped against the corner of the couch, weak and played out. As she raised her head, the cushion wadded up in her arms, her eyes went to the spot in front of the fireplace where all this had started sixteen years ago. Night was falling, and the only light came from the lamp on the table beside the couch, so the half-lit room didn't look too different from the way it had looked that Christmas Eve.

Tonight, that moment was hard to picture.

It had been a fact of life for so long, and she'd told the story so many times, maybe it was the story she remembered more than the event.

Tears threatened again. Mandy bit her lip.

*Is it worth it?*

Sixteen years of believing in a man in a crimson suit when everyone else thought she'd imagined it. Sixteen years of trying to hold on to the magic. Maybe by now, it was more stubbornness than belief. Maybe it had been for a long time.

Maybe it was time to let it go.

She remembered another night when she'd felt this way. Mandy shoved the thought aside. She was depressed enough already.

She pushed herself off the couch. No more thinking tonight. She headed to the kitchen for something to eat or drink.

Feeling like the world's biggest cliché, she dug a carton of ice cream out of the freezer and carried it back to the living room, preparing to pick out a movie from the top shelf of her cabinet.


If this were a Humphrey Bogart film, Jake thought, he would have been sitting at a bar, knocking back shots of whiskey.

Instead, he sat huddled at a table in the Pine 'n' Dine, his hands clutched around a cup of coffee. His mind swirled.

*My girlfriend is Joan of Arc. Only with Santa Claus.*

Jake took another swig of coffee and wished the world made sense again. On the one hand, Mandy's revelation explained a lot of things. The secretive behavior. The weird conversation about ghosts in the kitchen.

He should be saying, *Is that all?*

As secrets went, it could be so much worse. She didn't have a husband lurking around, or a baby he didn't know about. She could have been a felon. Or there were people who thought they'd been abducted by aliens.

She just believed in Santa Claus.

In a way, it made sense. It fit Mandy, with her air of innocence, her love for Christmas, her sweet disposition. But it might suggest a pretty shaky grip on reality.

And he was sitting here because *she* didn't want to talk to *him*.

"I haven't seen you in a while."

The red-haired waitress named Sherry stood in front of him, order pad in hand, an unspoken question on her face. Maybe she just wanted to know his order, but he didn't think so.

He'd driven around for over an hour, hoping in vain for everything to come clear for him. He supposed it was no accident he'd ended up at this particular restaurant. It was Sherry who'd first popped off with the nickname "Mandy Claus." Sherry must know all about this.

Jake flipped open his menu as if it held the answer to some trick question. "Uh—ham and cheese on rye."

Sherry sidled away.

Jake looked at his watch. Seven-thirty here, ten-thirty on the East Coast. He should be hungry, but he wasn't. He shouldn't be exhausted, but he was.

He'd only taken one semester of psychology, but he kept searching for explanations, and the amateur Freud in him whispered insistently about abandonment issues. The fact that her father had left that same year just seemed too significant. Maybe Santa Claus represented the ultimate father figure—kind, all-knowing, and with one heck of a good excuse for being gone all the time.

Before Jake could stretch his lame attempt at a theory any further, Sherry brought his sandwich, with a big side order of curiosity visible on her face. Maybe he could indulge her curiosity and get some answers in the bargain. The restaurant was busy, but judging from her expression, Jake had a feeling she'd make time for a few questions.

He cut to the chase. "So," he said, "you know about Mandy and Santa Claus?"

Her eyes flickered. "Do you?"

*Give me a break.* "You're the one who called her Mandy Claus."

"A lot of people do. It's just a nickname."

He sighed. The dinner crowd wouldn't allow for beating around the bush. "Sherry, she told me all about it. Why the tap dance?"

Sherry blinked. "What did she tell you?"

"That she saw Santa Claus when she was eight. Isn't that what she told you?"

"Sure. But she told me not to tell you."

He didn't want to put his foot in his mouth again, so he proceeded with caution. "Do you believe it?" he asked. Maybe there was something in the water here.

"That she saw Santa?" She stared at him. "Of course not. That's crazy."

Jake flinched. At least he hadn't used *that* word. But still, his reaction must have hit Mandy like a slap in the face. As he opened his mouth to speak in her defense, Sherry turned toward the kitchen. "Be back in a minute."

Jake tried to eat, but the sandwich held about as much interest as a bowl of wax fruit.

When Sherry returned, he didn't waste any time. "You know she's not crazy."

"I didn't say *Mandy* was crazy. Believing in Santa Claus is crazy. As far as I know she's totally normal in every other way."

"And everybody knows about this but me?"

"Well, you're new around here," Sherry said. "And it was summer when you came. And she asked me not to tell." She shrugged. "I don't know if she asked anybody else."

"Why would she try so hard to keep it from me if everybody knows about it?"

He knew the answer before Sherry spoke. She asked, "How did you take it?"

"Never mind." He swiped his hand through his hair. "I'm still trying to get my head around it. I heard how she saw Santa Claus. How'd everyone else find out?"

"It was a big deal," Sherry said. "Big for Tall Pine, anyway. She talked to a TV reporter, got her picture in the paper, all that stuff. And the kids at school made fun of her."

"Including you?"

"Well . . . yes." Sherry reddened. "But that was a long time ago. Remember, I was a kid, too."

Kids could be awful. Jake remembered that from trying to fit in at new schools while his family moved around. But adults should know better. "This Mandy Claus nickname," he said. "You know it hurts her feelings, right?"

Sherry gave him what looked like an honest-to-goodness double take. "No. Everybody loves Mandy. We've always kidded her about it, but it doesn't bother her. Not since she was little, anyway."

They stared at each other. One of them was way off.

Jake heard Mandy's voice in his head: *I can take it from everyone else.* His stomach twisted.

"See, what happened was . . ." Sherry looked upward in thought. "At first, when the kids teased her, she argued and cried. But then, it was funny— she just stopped arguing. She'd shrug her shoulders, or she'd laugh it off. She was like Teflon. A lot of backbone, that girl."

Sherry glanced toward the waiting area as a new set of customers walked in. "The thing is, she tells that story to any kid who walks in the store if they ask. The other store owners all know about it, and they send the kids over. It's like a tradition." Her eyes zeroed in on him. "Why would she do all that—why would she go to work in a Christmas store—if it still bothered her?"

*Good question,* he thought. *I'll have to ask her. If she'll speak to me.*

"She doesn't make a big deal of it," Sherry went on. "She doesn't take out a billboard. But everybody knows this town wouldn't be the same without her."

She tore off Jake's ticket and laid it on the table, although he'd barely touched his food. She started to walk away. Then she took a step back.

"If she was worried about you knowing, it's a big

deal to her," Sherry said. "So don't *you* hurt her feelings. Or else."

When Mandy heard the footsteps on her front porch, something loosened in her chest, and she knew she'd been waiting for the sound.

She reached for the remote control in the dark living room and paused the movie to listen. The steps came again, followed by a knock, and her insides tightened once more. She wasn't ready. She didn't know if she'd ever be ready.

She opened the door. Jake stood outside, wearing the blue jacket she'd bought him. Part of her wanted to launch into his arms, and that part terrified her. She was weak tonight. Weak enough that earlier, she'd been thinking of giving up everything she'd believed since she was a little girl.

She didn't trust herself, so she didn't open the door all the way.

Jake inclined his head to peer past her at the glow from the television screen. "What are you watching?"

*"The Godfather."*

He gave a faint smile. "That sounds ominous."

At that smile, something caught in her throat. She didn't answer.

Jake huddled deeper in his jacket, and Mandy

felt the bite of the air coming through the gap in the door. "Mind if I come in?" he asked.

She clutched the doorjamb. "I'm sorry, Jake. But I don't know if I'm ready to talk."

"I think we ought to." He passed a hand roughly through his hair, a familiar gesture that made him look rumpled and vulnerable. Mandy tightened her grip on the doorjamb.

Candid brown eyes met hers under the porch light. She was shaking. *Have some guts,* she told herself. *It can't be any worse than sitting alone in the dark having Häagen-Dazs for dinner.*

"Okay." Rather than let him in, she grabbed the sweater she'd thrown on the back of the couch and slipped through the door into the cold air outside.

He stared at her. "You really like to have an exit strategy, don't you?"

"What?" She pulled on the sweater. It didn't do much to guard against the chill.

"Never mind."

So now she had both of them standing outside in the bitter October night. Her knees were knocking. Let Jake think it was just from the cold. Mandy wrapped her arms around herself, under the sweater, and waited, afraid to speak.

Jake plunged ahead. "Mandy, I know I said everything wrong earlier tonight. I stepped on something really important to you. I hurt your feelings. And I'm sorry." He toed a board on the porch, his eyes still on hers. "What I want more than anything is just to get back to where we were."

"You mean, before I told you?" Her heart was in her throat. "I don't know if we can."

"Why not? I'm trying to tell you *it doesn't matter.*"

She stiffened. "It matters to me."

"I know it does. What I mean is, I don't have a problem with it."

She knew he intended for that to be good news. It might be the best she could hope for. But her heart sank at the thought. *Stand your ground,* something deep inside her insisted.

"Mandy, I'm lost. What can I do to make this better?"

"I don't want you to *overlook* it." She looked down. "I guess I hoped you'd believe me."

"I believe *you* believe it. Isn't that enough? It's not like it's a religious difference."

"Isn't it?" she said. "Faith is evidence of things unseen."

"Right. But . . ." He raked a hand through his hair again. "This is the deal-breaker? Really? Because I don't have an answer for that. Except that I've always told you the truth. I'm telling you the truth right now. If you expect me to turn around and say I believe in Santa Claus . . ."

She clutched her arms tighter around herself. "I've always hoped there was someone else who believed it. Maybe even someone else who saw him, too."

Jake gave a heavy sigh. "Now, *that* would be some fierce competition. But if there *is* a guy like that out there, I don't know where he is. Maybe he's ninety years old. Maybe he's in Denmark. Or maybe he's already married with eight tiny reindeer. I don't know." Jake leveled his direct gaze at her. "Here's what I *do* know. He didn't fly out here today to see you. He didn't drive to your store without stopping. He's not standing out here on your front porch, freezing. Doesn't any of that tell you anything?"

His words seemed to hang in the cold air between them. He was angry, he was impatient, but he was *here*.

Mandy gulped. "It means a lot."

He was right. She wasn't being fair. And, she realized, she still wasn't being honest. She owed him that much. She pulled in a deep breath and willed tears back.

*I've always told you the truth. . . .*

She dug deep and tried to find a way to explain why it mattered so much.

When she forced the words out, what finally came was: "Jake, I'm scared."

"You're what?" The anger seemed to drain away as his eyes searched hers.

She lowered her eyes. "I'm afraid—if I'm with someone who doesn't believe me, after a while I'll stop believing it myself."

She didn't dare look at him. Her legs rattled with a life all their own.

"Hey." She felt his hands on her shoulders, and that made her want to cry even more. "I'm not asking you to do that."

"I know. But you're so . . . realistic."

"You make it sound dirty."

She let out a shaky laugh. "Really. Think about it." She spoke through a huge ache in her throat. "If it wasn't my imagination, I *can't* be the only person this ever happened to. Where are the others?" She peered up at a blurry Jake. "I think most of them stopped believing it a long time ago. A lot of them probably right away, when they were kids, when people told them it couldn't be real. And the rest . . . maybe just bit by bit . . ." She swallowed hard. "On nights like this it's really hard for me to keep believing it. Like after my mom died—"

"—and you went to Mount Douglas."

"Right." Heaven help her, sometimes he did understand her. She blinked, and thank goodness, the tears stayed back. Her vision cleared, giving her a better view of Jake and his searching eyes.

Gently, he squeezed her shoulders, making her want to trust him, want to lean on him. That might be even scarier. "What happens if you stop believing?" he asked softly.

"Then there's no magic," she whispered. "And I've probably been crazy all this time."

"Mandy," he said, "I'm a logical guy. I admit it. That's why I acted the way I did earlier tonight. But there's nothing wrong with you. I know that." He reached up and traced her cheek with the outside of his fingers. "Guys like me look for reasons. We look for explanations. I've been trying for hours to make sense out of this, and I only know two things. When it comes to you and Santa Claus, 'sense' doesn't work. And I love you."

Mandy swayed on her feet. She didn't know what to say. But she was afraid if she gave in now, she'd be giving up a piece of herself.

*What are you talking about? You told him you believe in Santa Claus. And he's still here.*

Jake's eyes didn't leave her face. "All I'm saying is I want to be with you. Who knows? Maybe this whole deal will fall apart, Regal Hotels will toss me out on my ear, and I'll end up homeless. I'll be the crazy street guy of Tall Pine, and you'll be the normal one."

*Hold your ground,* a voice in her head insisted. *If there's one person in the world who's got to believe you, it's—*

Jake reached up and cupped her face in his hands. They were ice-cold.

But when he kissed her, his lips were warm. Mandy felt herself melting, and the little flashing warning light in her mind grew dimmer, the part of her that wasn't sure if this was good or bad.

An icy gust blew straight into them, drawing them closer together. Mandy held on to Jake and stopped thinking about good or bad. Stopped thinking about anything. There was only this moment and the solid, reassuring feeling of being in his arms.

Jake broke the kiss and pulled her tighter against him. The wind bit his face. *They're going to find us out here in the morning,* his jet-lagged brain said. *A statue of two icicle people.*

He opened his eyes and saw two small flecks of white on his jacket sleeve. No, it couldn't be. He wasn't one for magical signs, but . . .

"Mandy?"

"Mm?" Her face was snuggled into the shoulder of his jacket, whether for comfort or for warmth, he wasn't sure.

"Does it really snow here in October?"

She pulled back. "No. It never snows before Thanksgiving. It—"

The flecks were swirling around them now, blown toward the front of the house by the wind, flickering in the illumination of her porch light. Mandy tilted her face upward, letting the flakes fall on her cheeks.

A smile spread slowly across her face, and it was absolutely radiant.

# Chapter 14

As soon as they were inside, Mandy went to the window to pull the curtains open, letting in a view of the snowfall. Jake remembered she'd told him how excited Southern Californians got about snow. Tonight, he couldn't blame her. One freak October snow flurry couldn't solve everything. But it had come at the right time, lightening the mood, and the flakes swirling in the darkness outside were dazzling to look at.

Jake joined her at the window and put his arm around her. "Do you have any wood?" he asked. "I could build a fire."

"There's a wood pile behind the house." Hesitation flickered in her eyes. "But you've been out in the cold enough for one night."

Her answer gave him an out, but she didn't quite tell him *not* to do it. "I don't mind." He lifted a strand of her hair with fingers that were still numb. "Show me where it is, before I thaw out."

"I'll make hot chocolate," she offered.

"Deal." He grinned. "Or I could make the cocoa, and you could carry the firewood."

Mandy lifted her chin. "We'll compromise. Come on."

She guided him to the back door just off the kitchen and started to lead the way outside. Jake stopped her with a hand on her arm, gently pushing her back into the house. "It's okay. Just point the way."

"You're sure?"

"Yes. It's a guy thing. And you'd better close the door before you let all the cold inside."

After Mandy went in, he made his way briskly down a set of wooden steps toward the woodpile. The house blocked the wind on this side, but the cold still seized around him as if it had missed him during his brief absence. A guy thing, indeed. What else besides macho chivalry could possess him to volunteer to come back out into this? It *had* to be true love.

Without the wind to carry them, the snowflakes fell straighter on this side of the house. They still seemed fairly sparse. Fortunately, that also meant they hadn't done much to dampen the wood. Jake grabbed a quick armload and vaulted back up the steps as fast as his cargo would allow.

He walked through the kitchen past Mandy, diligently at work with a saucepan on the stove, and

**193**

made straight for the fireplace. By the time she entered the living room carrying two mugs, he'd coaxed the wood into a respectable blaze.

She raised her eyebrows and nodded at the flames. "You're pretty good at that."

"I'd better be." Jake got up from his kneeling position, brushing his hands off on his slacks. "Remember, I grew up back east."

Mandy set the two oversized mugs on the end of the coffee table closest to the fire, and they settled on the couch to watch the drifting flakes through the front window. Jake circled his arm around her shoulders, savoring her warmth as much as the heat from the flames.

"It probably won't last long," she said. "It's too early in the year."

Jake sipped from his mug. The rich flavor didn't taste anything like the instant packets he was used to. "What's in this?"

"Real chocolate. Condensed milk. Vanilla. And a little cinnamon."

"You had all that stuff in the kitchen?"

"It's always good to be prepared."

Jake took another sip, letting the cocoa seep into him as the fire brought back some of the circulation to his legs and feet.

"I missed you," Mandy said.

"It's good to be back."

He hoped things between them were finally back

where they'd been when he arrived this afternoon. The night had taken a dramatic turn for the better, and Jake was reluctant to question it. It also felt fragile, like a branch that it might not be smart to put too much weight on just yet. So he tried for a lighter note.

He glanced at the now-blank television screen. "Can I ask you a question?"

"What?" she asked.

"Why *The Godfather*?"

"Well, number one, it's a great story."

"I agree. Now, what's the other reason?"

She blew into her cocoa, avoiding his eyes. "I love Al Pacino in it. He starts out so vulnerable. I know where he's headed, but I still enjoy watching it."

She cupped her cocoa mug, still gazing into the drink. "I'm sorry about all the drama," she said. "I kept stalling, waiting for a good time to tell you. . . ."

He pressed his lips to her brow. "Don't worry about it."

She rested her cheek against his shoulder, and Jake relished the feel of it. He was, he realized, bone tired, and he would have been happy to stay in this spot for the next several hours without moving. The cocoa warmed him from the inside, and he felt a deepening sense of contentment.

After a few minutes, however, he sensed a quiet shift in Mandy's mood. He couldn't see what she was looking at, or even whether her eyes were open, but he realized her head wasn't turned toward the window anymore.

If he had to guess, her eyes were directed at the floor in front of the fireplace.

Jake considered the spot. It wasn't a traditional raised hearth; only a flat area of brick created a safe amount of space between the screened-in flames and the carpet. As firelight flickered over the floor, the space did seem to take on a magical look. He tried to imagine what she was seeing.

"This is where it happened?" he asked. "Right here in front of the fireplace?"

Her head stirred on his shoulder. "Are you trying to humor me?"

"No. I want to be able to see it. To picture it," he amended.

"You heard me tell the story."

"I heard you tell it to the little boy in the store," Jake said. "But I've told quite a few stories to Emily, and if you're like me—well, stories get refined over time. Like the way you used those lines from 'The Night Before Christmas.'"

"It's called 'A Visit from St. Nicholas,' actually."

He had no doubt she knew the poem by heart. "Right. So tell me the way *you* saw it."

She raised her head from his shoulder. "Seriously?"

"Seriously."

Mandy straightened, drawing back to look at

him. She'd never had an adult ask her this, ever. But Jake appeared to be sincere. He didn't look as if he meant to deconstruct her story like some armchair CSI investigator.

She closed her eyes and thought. "Okay. I sneaked out of bed after my mom was done wrapping presents, and I stretched out here on the couch to wait. My head was at that end." She nodded toward the far side of the couch. "It was after eleven, and I did fall asleep. But when I woke up, it was like something startled me awake. You know how sometimes you hear a noise in your sleep, and you don't know what woke you up until you hear it again? It was like that. And I was *wide*-awake. I remember my heart was beating faster."

She looked toward the window. This time, she didn't see the snow. She was picturing the Christmas tree in the spot where she still put it up year after year. "This room gets pretty bright at night at Christmas, when the tree is lit. My mom always used white lights for the tree. I tried colored lights once, and they were pretty, but they weren't the same. The white lights are more like candlelight."

She turned her head toward the fireplace. "So, I looked over there—we had lights around the outside edges of the fireplace, too. I just remembered that." She traced the shape of the fireplace in the air with her finger. "And he was there. Not a silhouette, not a shadow. I could see his face. Part of me wants to say he was carrying a bag over his shoulder, but I'm not sure."

"What did he look like?"

"I remember two things really well: the color of his suit, and his expression. His clothes weren't bright red. They're a deeper color, more of a crimson. But I don't think I thought of that word then. What I remember most is his face. That's why I complain about the store Santas, because it's so hard to describe. He looked serious—but not *stern*, like some of those old English Santas. He had a glimmer in his eye, but not a *ho-ho-ho* look like most of the American Santas. I don't think he was smiling, but maybe with the beard, it was just hard to tell."

She waited, afraid he'd ask her if she'd known anyone who looked like that, relieved when he didn't.

"And the flash of light when he left—that's absolutely true. There's no way he just walked out the door. He wasn't some guy dressed up."

Mandy tried to think of other details to add, but nothing came to mind. She contemplated the spot in front of them. She and Jake were sitting closer to the hearth than she had been that night, and the fire Jake had built cast its flickering patterns on the bricks. But her mind's eye was seeing something else. The image of that long-ago night, the one she'd struggled so hard to capture a couple of hours ago, came clear. The kind face, the sense of peace and wonder. She drew in a slow breath, almost afraid to look away. But she turned to Jake.

He was looking, not at the fireplace, but at her, his features quiet and thoughtful. Thoughtful, she hoped, and not analytical.

When her eyes met his, he smiled and nodded toward the fireplace. "You really know how to paint a picture."

As if, in some way, he saw it too. She knew he couldn't *see* it, see it, the way she had. The way she could picture it now. But he wasn't trying to drag in logic this time, and if she was reading his expression right, he wasn't just playing along either. She had the feeling she'd had about Jake before—that maybe, in some small way, he *got* it.

Maybe that was enough.

For tonight, her own mental picture was clear again, and that helped. It had been her anchor, the thing she'd clung to, all these years. But maybe there were other things to believe in.

She set her cocoa mug on the coffee table next to Jake's. It was still more than half-full; somewhere along the line, he'd emptied his. Turning to Jake, she put a hand on his cheek. He'd shaved since this afternoon, long ago enough now that she could feel a hint of stubble starting to return. It had been that many hours since he'd gotten back to town. She looked past Jake to the mantel clock.

It was nearly midnight—three hours later on the East Coast. With the travel, the time zones, and everything that had happened since he arrived, he must be worn out.

"You really didn't know what you were getting into with me," she said. "I'm sorry."

"I'm not." He covered her hand on his cheek with his own. "I got a lot more than I bargained for. But that's a good thing."

Jake looked down at Mandy's face in the firelight. He didn't know if he believed in Santa Claus, but the soft glow of those blue eyes made it a lot easier to believe in peace on earth, good will toward men. Whatever she'd seen that night had been real enough to her. And hearing her recall it in such calm, clear-eyed detail filled him not with worry, but with wonder.

"I meant what I said." He curled his fingers around hers. "I'm in love with you. I don't know what's going to happen yet with this hotel mess, but—"

"I love you, too," she said, and reached up to kiss him, as if she'd had enough words for tonight.

And had he just called his job a *mess*?

Didn't matter. As their lips met, he drew Mandy against him. It was a hot-chocolate-flavored kiss, perfect for an impossibly snowy mid-October night. Dimly he realized he wasn't sure if it was still snowing or not. That didn't matter either.

Just a little earlier he'd been exhausted, but not now. The warmth between them coursed through him like a reviving current.

Mandy's arms were around his neck, her lips soft, yielding, giving. Jake brought his hand up to tunnel his fingers though her hair, his arm around her waist drawing her closer, trying to close any space between them. As he kissed her again, he nibbled lightly on her bottom lip, and she made a tiny sound from the back of her throat that threatened to be his undoing. He let his lips wander across her cheek and down the side of her neck, relishing the warmth of her skin and the scent of her hair. Her sigh filled his ears, and tantalizing thoughts flooded his mind.

He didn't want to go anywhere. He would have loved to stay here all night, for so many reasons, not the least of which was the inviting way Mandy's body felt pressed against his.

But there were so many reasons not to. After tonight, he was sure of what he'd suspected all along: Mandy had never slept with anyone. It wasn't something Jake entered into lightly either. Spending the night with her while his work was still so uncertain, knowing that soon he might have to leave for good, wouldn't be right.

It wouldn't be right under any circumstances, he realized. Because Mandy Reese was a forever girl.

And forever wasn't something he could promise. Not yet.

Jake raised his head, wondering if this was the way the earth would feel if it tried to resist the pull of its orbit around the sun. As he looked down at her, Mandy's eyes were shining, heavy-lidded and impossible to resist. He dipped his head down for another kiss, then another.

He didn't want to stop. And he really needed to.

Mandy savored Jake's arms around her, the feeling of being so totally enfolded. When he raised his head, she didn't want him to stop; when he didn't kiss her, it felt like slowly waking up. Reluctantly she loosened the hold of her arms around him. There was something solemn in his face as he looked down at her. He traced the outline of her lips with one fingertip. Mandy shivered.

"Ever wish you could freeze time?" he asked.

She willed herself to form words. "Sometimes. Why?"

"I was just thinking this would be a good moment." His finger continued its slow, lazy trail along the bottom of her lower lip. "I wouldn't have to move from this spot. . . ."

She waited, not sure where he was going with the thought, only sure that the feather-light touch of his fingertip was making her crazy.

"But I'd better go now," he said.

She hadn't expected to hear *that.*

For the moment, at least, Jake didn't move. "Tomorrow's Sunday," he said. "You're off, right?"

"Of course. The store's closed Sunday."

"You and two-thirds of Tall Pine. Okay, what I'd like to do—" His lips brushed briefly over hers again. "Scratch that. What I *need* to do is go and get a decent night's sleep. Then call you in the morning and spend every waking minute with you. If you don't mind."

"That sounds wonderful."

"Then, Monday, the real fun starts," he said. "First thing in the morning, I have breakfast with Winston Frazier. And try to convince him I'm not the devil."

# Chapter 15

"A poached egg, orange juice, and a slice of dry toast." Winston Frazier handed his menu to the waitress at the Pine 'n' Dine, a young brunette Jake didn't recognize. Her name tag said *Tiffany*.

"A Belgian waffle, a side of bacon, and a cup of coffee, please," Jake said.

Already, they were opposites. Tiffany left, and it was time for the small talk. Frazier surprised Jake by starting it off. "So how was New York?"

"Pennsylvania."

"Pennsylvania." A flicker in Frazier's slate-gray eyes suggested, *Same thing*.

"Busy," Jake said. "And warmer than here."

"Yes, we've had quite a cold snap," Frazier acknowledged.

"What I really didn't expect was the snow."

Frazier looked at him quizzically. "Snow?"

"Saturday night." Jake frowned. "There was even a little left over in the trees Sunday morning."

Frazier shook his head slowly. "I was up at five a.m. Sunday. I didn't see a thing."

Okay, weather could be pretty localized. Come to think of it, Jake hadn't noticed any evidence of snow around his hotel either, and that was barely five minutes from Mandy's house. But the blue spruce in her tiny front yard had definitely worn a sprinkling of white yesterday morning.

As their food arrived, Jake's cell phone chirped in his pocket. He grimaced inwardly as he brought it out and muted it. He'd thought the diner, like so much of Tall Pine, was in a dead spot.

"Sorry." He pocketed the phone again. "Forgot to turn it off."

Frazier eyed him curiously. "Aren't you going to check it?"

"Not unless it's from you, and that doesn't seem likely." Jake reached for his coffee. "If it's important, they left a message. I'm with who I'm with."

He'd learned that lesson the hard way, on his first project five years ago in Philadelphia, but Frazier didn't need to know that part. He was still studying Jake with a faint air of reassessment. Maybe having his phone go off hadn't been such an unlucky thing after all.

"So," Jake said, "I came to hear your thoughts about the hotel project."

"I think you have a fair idea of where we stand," Frazier said. "So far Tall Pine's managed to keep out the corporate chains they've got everywhere else in Southern California. This is nothing personal. It's the Regal Hotel chain, in principle, that we have a problem with."

Jake wondered how many people he was including in that "we."

"Understood." Jake's response brought a lift of Frazier's eyebrows. "I can see what you want to preserve. Tall Pine is a beautiful, quiet community. That's what visitors come here for. But there's no denying your town relies on the tourist trade. . . ."

Frazier's eyes took on a blank, polite stare that told Jake he was tuning out. Jake was talking too much again, he realized. And the whole purpose of this meeting was to *not* recreate the town council meeting.

Jake shifted gears. "Sorry. You've heard my spiel. What am I doing wrong?"

"Aside from trying to rebuild a place as soon as you get here?"

*Hey, it's my job.* But Jake held his tongue.

"You've tried to make yourself at home too fast. We've all seen you around, trying to soak up local color. You probably mean well. But getting to know a place like this—it doesn't happen all at once. Some people might even think you're using Mandy Reese."

As Jake lifted his cup, hot coffee sloshed onto his hand. "What?"

Frazier sliced into the flavorless-looking egg on his plate. "You take up with a local girl, learn about the town from her. Maybe you even think the council will look at you more kindly with her sitting next to you." He shrugged. "People might think you were trying to do that."

Inside, Jake sizzled. But when he answered, he kept his voice level. "They would be wrong."

While Jake counted to ten in his head, Frazier calmly took another bite, letting the ball take another bounce in Jake's court. This felt a whole lot like a test. If Jake argued too vehemently, it could sound like he was protesting too much.

But Jake had spent the first half of his childhood being the new kid in town. He'd learned that sometimes you had to roll with the punches. And sometimes you had to stand firm.

"The fact is," Jake said, "Mandy is reason enough for me to want to stick it out here. The company probably wouldn't mind if I let this one go. The funny thing is, I think Tall Pine would be a pretty friendly place if I were here for any other reason."

"Possibly."

Jake met Frazier's slate-gray eyes. "So," he said, "since this isn't personal, tell me more about your concerns."

\* \* \*

The bells on the shop door jingled just before five, and Mandy looked up from the register to see Jake in his polo shirt and the navy windbreaker.

Mrs. Swanson, on her way to the door to turn around the *Closed* sign, greeted him first. "Welcome back."

"Thanks. That's good to hear."

There seemed to be an extra layer of gratitude in his voice, and he looked tired. Mandy closed the register, walked up and greeted him with a hug. "How'd the breakfast meeting go?"

"Interesting. I'll fill you in once you're free."

"I was just getting ready to count out the register." Mandy rounded the counter, opened the register and pulled out the cash tray. "I'll be ready in fifteen minutes."

As she moved toward the back room to count the money, she was aware of Mrs. Swanson's eyes going from her to Jake. The woman didn't miss much, and Mandy had the feeling she was measuring the degrees of warmth between the two of them.

Behind her, she heard Jake asking Mrs. Swanson, "Did you get any snow Saturday night?"

Mandy could almost hear her boss's puzzled frown. "No. It never snows here before Thanksgiving."

"That's what people keep telling me," Jake said.

\* \* \*

When Mrs. Swanson left, Mandy was still in back counting out the cash drawer, so Jake sauntered through the shop. The displays had shifted quite a bit since he'd been gone. He noticed a small section of turkeys and pilgrims alongside the fall pumpkins and jack-o'-lanterns, waiting for their turn on center stage of the off-season table. Then his eyes wandered to the south wall of the store, where a pair of matching frames—one red, one green—caught his eye. He didn't think they'd been there before. Inside the frames, he saw two cleanly reproduced newspaper clippings.

Jake strolled over to take a look. The red-framed clipping on the left showed the profile of a dark-haired little girl with a microphone held in front of her by someone who wasn't in the shot. The headline read, *TRUE BELIEVER: LOCAL FOURTH GRADER SAW SANTA CLAUS.*

The article elaborated:

> By fourth grade, most children are pretty doubtful about old St. Nick. But a television reporter interviewing children at Tall Pine Elementary got a refreshing eyewitness account from nine-year-old Mandy Reese, who says she saw Santa Claus at her home last year. . . .

Jake noticed the article didn't include an interview with Mandy, just a retelling of her earlier interview with the television reporter. The green-framed article on the right featured a very recognizable photograph of Mandy standing behind the counter of The North Pole, smiling shyly. *SANTA SIGHTER GOES TO WORK AT CHRISTMAS STORE.*

> The North Pole has a new helper to spread the Christmas spirit.
> The Christmas store on Evergreen Lane, which specializes in yuletide items year-round, has hired Mandy Reese, a recent graduate of Tall Pine High School. Many locals will remember the 18-year-old as the 9-year-old who told television reporters she saw Santa Claus tiptoe through her living room on Christmas Eve. . . .

The piece went on to quote Mrs. Swanson at length, describing her new employee as "a natural" and hedging somewhat about the store's past struggles to stay afloat with the previous owner.

> Asked if she still believes in Santa, Reese's eyes took on a playful sparkle.
> "Of course," she said. "Doesn't everyone?"

A smile twitched at Jake's lips. Not exactly hard-hitting journalism, but a small-town newspaper could do worse.

"Oh," Mandy said from behind him. "You found them. That didn't take long."

"The frames caught my eye. Where were they before?"

"Behind the counter. I sort of accidentally-on-purpose dropped one a few months ago."

"Because of me?"

She nodded.

Jake gestured toward the second article. "You don't say much in here."

"I was eighteen. And I felt so awkward. Mrs. Swanson did most of the talking. I felt like a prize cow."

Jake put his arm around her shoulders. "She knows you're more than that. You know that, don't you?"

"I do now. She's been really good to me."

He thought back to his conversation with Winston Frazier this morning, and with Sherry the other night. It seemed to him a whole lot of people knew Mandy was special. And she seemed so unaware of it herself.

He turned her to face him. "You amaze me."

And before she could ask him a silly question like why, he kissed her.

Mandy lowered her eyes, fingering his collar. "Now tell me about your meeting."

"Oh. That." He clasped his hands loosely around her waist. "It's a tough one to call. Frazier definitely doesn't love the idea. And my phone went off right when we were starting. I was afraid—"

It occurred to him he hadn't seen a message when he checked his phone after the meeting. He pulled it out to look again. No notification of a voice mail, and the first text he'd received hadn't come until after breakfast.

He frowned. "You weren't trying to call me, were you?"

"No. And I sure wouldn't have tried you during . . ."

Jake's frown deepened as he scrolled over the phone's screen.

"What is it?" Mandy asked.

"Nothing," he said. "Literally nothing. No text, nothing on the Missed Calls log . . ." He shrugged and re-pocketed his phone. "Weird."

Phantom cell phone calls, highly localized snowfall . . . he was starting to wonder if he'd fallen into the Twilight Zone. But it seemed to be working for the good, so maybe he just shouldn't question it.

Mandy's voice pulled him back from his thoughts. "So what did Winston say?"

"Kind of a compromise. He says he's going to make sure the public knows the item's coming up at the next town council meeting, so they can fire all their questions at me."

"That's Wednesday, right?"

"I know. Two nights from now. I'm not sure how he's going to rearrange the laws of space and time, but—"

Jake's cell phone rang in his pocket. With a faint air of premonition, he fished it out, one arm still around Mandy. "Jake Wyndham."

"Mr. Wyndham, this is Bret Radner with the *Tall Pine Gazette*."

Jake glanced at the byline on Mandy's two articles. No Radner up there. Of course, this wouldn't be one of those sweet human-interest stories. But two minutes later, Jake had agreed to meet the reporter for an interview back at the cafe where he'd met with Frazier that morning.

Hanging up, he looked at Mandy apologetically. "I'm sorry. Dinner plans are on hold. Guess who's being interviewed for tomorrow's paper."

"You're kidding. That's awfully tight."

"Well, they manage it for the local football scores, don't they?"

"Only if the games don't go into overtime."

Moments later, he was out the door, wondering just what he was headed for. Jake remembered breakfast again. Then he thought back to his first conversation with Mrs. Swanson. She hadn't said much, but basically, she'd warned him to be good to Mandy.

He thought of Sherry, half-joking: *Don't* you *hurt her feelings. Or else.*

And now, Winston Frazier. Whether Mandy realized it or not, people around here were pretty protective of her. Was Frazier looking out for Mandy? Or had he set up this newspaper interview to turn the crowd against him?

Either way, Jake figured he'd better be careful.

Bret Radner fell in line with Jake's idea of what a reporter should be, with a wiry build and sharp, dark eyes behind Clark-Kent-style glasses. He had a direct stare that made Jake want to ask if he had laser vision, except that with Radner's serious demeanor, that probably wouldn't go over. And when he wasn't asking questions, he didn't say much.

Okay, there were a few disappointing exceptions to the reporter cliché. No eye shade or suspenders, and he was at least twenty years too young—maybe younger than Jake himself. And he drank his coffee with cream, instead of black or laced with Jack Daniels. Of course, the latter wasn't exactly an option at the Pine 'n' Dine.

The questions so far had been aboveboard and detailed—far more detailed than Jake had gotten from the town council—including the proposed square footage of the hotel, number of units and possible traffic impact.

"I don't think anyone in Tall Pine really wants *less* traffic." Jake tried a smile. Nothing. The guy certainly got points for dogged professionalism, but Jake wondered if the article would end up as dry as Winston Frazier's toast. "My point is, I think the hotel will actually be good for traffic. The best proposed site is the old drive-in lot on the way out of town, farther up the mountain. It'd make one more stop for people to stay in Tall Pine instead of driving another forty-five minutes to Mount Douglas, so the location is really ideal."

Radner jotted rapidly into a small, narrow reporter's notebook, another item that fit the cliché to a T, and started the next question while he was still scrawling. "Locals are concerned that a chain hotel is a threat to the town's uniqueness. How do you answer that?"

By now, Jake could answer that one in his sleep. Trade-off, pros and cons, tourist business, controlled growth. He was starting to feel pretty good about the way this was going. But complacency was a dangerous thing.

Radner aimed a bespectacled stare at him, and somehow Jake knew this was it.

"Some people have expressed some concern about your relationship with Mandy Reese," Radner said.

Rats.

Jake met the reporter's eyes. "First, I'd like to go off the record for a minute."

He was gambling on the ethics of small-town

journalism, but this seemed like the best way to handle it, and everything about Bret Radner practically screamed *ethics*.

Radner gave a barely discernible nod, and his pen froze.

"The question puts me in a tight spot. Because I'm very serious about Miss Reese. But if I say that in print, it sounds like I'm trying to use that relationship for my own advancement."

Radner nodded again without comment. *He's not giving me any hints here.*

"Did you go to school with Mandy, by any chance?" Jake ventured.

"Irrelevant."

But Jake had a direct stare of his own. He used it.

"Two years ahead of her," Radner conceded. "But I'm not the one being interviewed." So the star reporter *was* younger than Jake.

Radner poised his pen, looked at Jake, and waited.

Jake sighed and forged ahead. "For the record . . ."


*"Until it was brought up to me, I'd never thought of the two together," Wyndham said carefully. "But yes, we're seeing each other, and no, it's not to give me any kind of an inside track to get the hotel approved. I wouldn't expect anyone to count it for me—or against me, for that matter.*

*The concern for Mandy has confirmed something for me, though. Tall Pine is definitely a town that looks out for its own."*

"'Carefully,'" Mandy echoed out loud. Elbows on the store counter, she lowered the newspaper to look at Jake. A sense of unease stole over her. "Why does he say 'carefully'?"

"Because that's the way I said it." Jake lifted the paper out of her hands gently. "Now I'm afraid I sounded too much like a politician."

Mandy frowned. "So, this means, what? They think you're using me to get on the town's good side?"

"Something like that." Jake shook out the paper, skimming down the page again. "It's not so bad. All the quotes are dead accurate, and the article's pretty even-handed. He quotes me; he quotes Frazier; he talks to Margery Williams. Pros and cons."

Jake's calm bewildered Mandy. And she couldn't believe she was in the paper again. At least she didn't have to worry about Mrs. Swanson hanging this one on the wall.

She sipped the Styrofoam cup of coffee Jake had brought in for her with the morning paper and made a face. She'd forgotten to put in cream and sugar.

She shook her head. "I don't get it. How would dating me make any difference?"

"Think about it. You've been working at The North Pole for, what? Six years? How many kids in town do you think you've told about Santa by now?"

Mandy tried to calculate. "Maybe one or two a month during the summer. At Christmastime . . ." She couldn't possibly count.

To her amazement, Jake was smiling. "While you weren't looking, you turned into an institution."

That was beyond comprehension. "So dating me is making problems for you?"

Jake set the paper down.

"Dating you," he said firmly, "is the best thing that ever happened to me. But if I say that, it sounds like I'm playing us up for the wrong reasons. I kept it as simple as I could. Now, either they believe me or they don't."

Her frown deepened. "What if they don't?"

"We'll cross that bridge when we come to it."

Mandy picked up the newspaper again, studying the printed words until the letters looked weird and squiggly. The idea that anyone was concerned about what she did, beyond her connection with Santa Claus and the Christmas store, baffled her. The idea that anyone would turn it against Jake—

"Doesn't this tick you off?" she asked.

"It did at first," he admitted. "But then I thought it over. This hubbub about you and me comes down to one of two things. It's either plain old soap opera mentality . . ." He shrugged.

"Or?"

"Or it's because they love you. And I can't blame them for that."

# Chapter 16

The last time Mandy walked into the lobby of the Tall Pine town hall, her stomach had been doing flip-flops. This time wasn't much different.

She cast a glance at the sign for the ladies' room as they passed it, remembering her emergency trip there. Okay, things were a little different. This time she and Jake were on the same page. She knew, wholeheartedly, that she wanted him to stay.

She closed her eyes and sent up a silent prayer, hoping once again that God understood incoherent shorthand. Then she opened her eyes before she could trip, and they walked into the council chambers.

They'd arrived early again, and the room was already as full as it had been when last month's meeting started. Jake steered them to the same seats they'd occupied before, in the center of the room, next to the podium.

"Are you sure this isn't bad luck?" she asked.

"I don't believe in luck," he said. "I do believe in being close to the podium."

Mandy slipped her hand into Jake's and watched the room fill. So many familiar faces. A few had been classmates, but most were older: customers, former teachers, shopkeepers from the other stores on Evergreen Lane. She saw Mrs. Swanson near the back. The chatter in the room slowly rose to a hum.

"How many people in Tall Pine?" she whispered to Jake. She knew he'd know.

"Nine thousand, eight hundred and seventy-three." He quirked a smile at her. "Think we need a few more chairs?"

A moment later, city staffers did, in fact, start to bring in extra folding chairs. Mandy's fingers tightened around Jake's. At a few minutes before six, Scotty Leroux took a spot leaning against the side wall rather than taking up another chair. He winked at her.

Finally, at seven minutes after six, the town council members filed in. Mandy loosened her grip on Jake's hand so he wouldn't have to pry himself free when he stood up.

The Regal Hotels project came first on the agenda. This time, Jake stepped to the podium in the same jacket and tie he'd worn on their first date. They were more formal than what the rest of the council wore, but he looked comfortable and

**221**

approachable. It wasn't just the council he had to sell tonight, though. The floor would be open for questions, and the room was packed. It was unfortunate that the podium was set up for Jake to face the council members rather than the audience.

As he started to speak, Mandy held her breath.

"Last time I was here," he said, "I made mistakes. I tried to tell your town council why a Regal Hotel would be good for your community. I tried to convince them that I understood what Tall Pine needed. But as one of your council members pointed out to me, no matter how hard I try, there's no way I can get to know your town overnight. Or even in a couple of months."

Then, to Mandy's surprise, he left the security of his podium and walked to the front of the room, a move she knew he hadn't planned. He leaned against the raised stage where the council members sat, angling himself so his back wasn't turned to the council completely, but so that he faced the crowd filling the chambers. Deep brown eyes surveyed the room, landing briefly on Mandy's, before he continued. Even without the microphone, his voice carried easily.

"Tonight the council's been gracious enough to allow me to come back and open the floor to the people this decision would really affect. And that's all of you. This time I'm here to listen, and to take your questions. So." He slapped the top of the stage with the palm of his hand as his eyes skimmed over the crowded council chambers. "Hit me."

For the next hour, Mandy watched Jake parry with the citizens of Tall Pine. He was nothing if not prepared. The hotter the hot seat got, the more relaxed Jake appeared. He came across as warm, personable and trustworthy, and he knew his figures backward and forward.

When the questions wound down, Jake addressed the group.

"I'll tell you the truth. Before I got here, Tall Pine was a dot on a map. Regal chose the town for its demographics, but we didn't know what it was like." Jake rested an elbow on the stage, his eyes sweeping slowly over the crowd to include everyone in the room. "That started to change as soon as I got out of my car. It's *different* here. You've got fresher air. You've got four-way stop signs that work. And don't tell my boss I said this, but I kind of love the fact that my cell phone is out of range three-quarters of the time. And I like walking into a store or a restaurant and feeling like I'm meeting someone who's going to remember me next time. You have something special here, and I think you can share it without turning Tall Pine into a metropolis."

"How do you propose we do that?" an audience member asked.

"That's in the hands of your town council. Up to now, Tall Pine hasn't had any concrete policies to prohibit national chain businesses. And up to now, you haven't needed that. Tradition's been enough. But the world's getting bigger all the time. Regal may have been the first national chain to approach the town, but we won't be the last. It's up to your council to set up policies and resolutions to control the amount of growth and the type of businesses you let in. I know they're equal to the task, because they know the value of what you have up here."

The council voted to have the committee evaluate Jake's responses to the public, and he braced himself for his next phone conversation with Mark. Jake knew Regal Hotels wouldn't be thrilled with another delay and another month of telecommuting. For his part, he counted the outcome as better than a draw.

The following week, the committee invited him to an informal meeting with them. The results of that meeting were less encouraging.

"They're snagging on one thing," he told Mandy as they tossed bread to the ducks at Prospect Lake. The wind coming off the lake was finger-numbingly cold, and Jake wondered why the birds hadn't flown south to Mexico. Or, at least, San Diego. "They're worried about the impact on the other hotels. I tried convincing them it would be apples and oranges, but they're afraid there won't be enough business to go around."

Mandy paused before tossing another piece of crust. "Unless."

Jake turned to her, eyebrows raised.

"What if you really made it apples and oranges?"

"Come again?"

"What if you gave the hotel a theme? I know I'm biased, but say, a Christmas theme. Something to make it more of a destination point, which the town would like. That could put it in a higher price bracket, so the other hotels would have the cost advantage."

He hesitated, crumbs in hand. "Regal's never done a theme hotel," he said slowly. "We're basic, we're reliable, we're affordable . . . but those things do make us more of a threat to the other hotels."

Jake stared out at the ducks, considering.

"It might work," he said slowly. "It's got points for originality. And it really could draw more tourists up here. It'd be good for everyone." He turned to Mandy. "You have an awesome brain."

"Thanks. I think."

Jake stared past the beautiful blue eyes in front of him, trying to see the proposal to Regal in his head. The more he thought about it, the better it sounded. It would attract a different type of vacationer than the existing hotels did, and the current hotel owners could still keep their share of business by continuing to offer a simple overnight stay at a lower price.

A theme hotel. Would Christmas be the right way to go?

"Although if I'm going to make it fly . . . maybe we could tone down the Christmas factor a little. Some people get maxed out on the holidays. If we did sort of a winter theme—pine trees, snowmen . . ."

Something in Mandy's eyes dimmed a little. "Like Christmas, but without the magic."

"Oh, I don't know. I hear those snowmen have been known to get up and dance around."

"Don't make fun."

*Note to self: Santa's real, but Frosty the Snowman is silly.*

"Sorry." He could run it by the Tall Pine committee first, then talk to Mark at the home office. . . .

"When did you stop believing?" Mandy asked.

Images of the committee faded, and Mandy came back into sharp focus in front of his eyes. She looked compassionate, almost pitying. But this could be thin ice. Jake stepped out on it cautiously.

"Second grade, I think. But it wasn't any big trauma. I guess I was always kind of suspicious. I was trying to hang tough, maybe because I was worried that if I stopped going along with it, the presents might stop too."

Her lips twitched upward. "Mercenary."

Okay, she did have a sense of humor about it. "So I was at the kitchen table writing up my *mercenary* Christmas list, and my brother Tony walked in. He's three years older. And, like any tactful big brother, he said, 'You don't really believe in that stuff, do you?'"

Mandy looked stricken. "That's terrible."

"It's what brothers do to each other. Although the youngest one never quite catches up. Tony has *still* hit me more times than I ever hit him. But we love each other."

"But he told you there was no Santa Claus. That's brutal."

"You're dealing with Mr. Practical, remember? After Tony talked to me, I did some independent research on my own. I finished my Christmas list that year. But then I made another one."

She frowned.

"One, I put on the refrigerator for my parents. The other one, I addressed to the North Pole and mailed it off without telling anyone." He shrugged. "Guess which list my presents came from."

"You *tested* Santa Claus?" She looked as if she wasn't sure whether to be horrified or amused.

"Scientific method."

This really *was* a little bit like a religious difference. He thought they'd better move on to a new topic.

Mandy persisted, "Let me ask you a question."

"Okay," he said cautiously.

"You're saying you got the presents you asked your parents for, right?"

"Right. I mean, not *everything*. But there was nothing from the Santa list."

"And which presents did you want more?"

"The ones on the fridge. I admit, I hedged my bets. But if you're saying Santa Claus had anything to do with what my parents bought me . . ."

She shrugged and smiled, amazingly placid. So Jake ventured one more step out on that thin ice.

"Then I should have gotten a lump of coal in my stocking, right? For testing Santa Claus."

"I never said he punishes bad kids. I don't know how it all works. I just know what I saw."

He'd made his peace with this, he reminded himself, and logic had nothing to do with it.

"Anyway," she said, "Christmas isn't about what's under the tree."

"You're right about that." He put his arm around her, his cheek resting on top of her head as he gazed over the lake. The evening sky was turning gray, and the wind was picking up, sending a bitter bite through his pullover. Winter would be here soon, and with it, Christmas.

A Christmas hotel. And suddenly he remembered an old Bing Crosby movie. "Mandy?"

"Hmm?" She sounded relaxed, contented.

"Were you by any chance thinking of *Holiday Inn* when you thought that up?"

"Maybe a little." He could hear the smile in her voice.

Yes, it could work. Regal Hotels wouldn't lose out on what they'd invested to send him out here. The other hotels wouldn't be threatened, the town would see more tourists, and he certainly had an expert consultant by his side. Plus, overseeing the opening of a themed hotel would undoubtedly take months longer, so Jake would be able to stay longer in Tall Pine.

Maybe even for good. He knew other Regal representatives who'd moved on to hotel management.

He pulled Mandy closer. One step at a time, he reminded himself. He had to get Tall Pine to say yes first, before he let himself think about . . .

The ducks and geese on the water had gotten subdued, their quacking silent, their movements lazy. Maybe because Jake and Mandy had stopped throwing food out on the water. Or maybe because it was darn cold out here.

Jake said, "This is a dangerous time of year for ducks, you know."

"Oh?"

"Sometimes it freezes when they're not ready for it. If the water turns to ice too fast, their legs get stuck under the surface—"

"Forget it." Mandy jabbed him in the ribs with her elbow, not too sharply. "I saw *Fried Green Tomatoes,* too."

For Mandy, November passed in a blur.

While she trained the three part-timers they'd hired for the Christmas rush, Jake met with the town council's hotel committee and kept Regal Hotels up-to-date on his progress. At last the committee held a meeting with the proprietors of the two local hotels. The hotel owners agreed that a holiday hotel wouldn't be likely to pull much of their existing business away. Jake spoke to Mark, his regional manager at Regal, who agreed the concept sounded promising. At Mark's recommendation, Jake started on a detailed proposal for the executive board.

And Mandy started on her first-ever yarn craft project: a needlepoint Christmas stocking for Jake.

The artwork in the predesigned kit actually included Santa Claus. With his face crafted in stitches, details were scant, so accuracy wasn't an issue. It showed Santa on top of a roof, the traditional pack on his back. Below the picture, just before the foot of the stocking began, needlepoint letters spelled out the word, *Believe.*

She hoped the message wouldn't seem heavy-handed. After all, *she* hadn't designed it.

The town council meeting the Wednesday night before Thanksgiving was very lightly attended, and Jake's time at the podium was short.

The council voted six to zero in favor of the proposed hotel, based on the holiday theme Jake described. Sitting alongside Jake in the same seat for the third time, Mandy saw his shoulders relax almost imperceptibly. And Mandy felt the butterflies in her stomach subside.

The next day, Mandy cooked Thanksgiving dinner at her house for Jake, Mrs. Swanson, and the three Christmas staffers. It was the first holiday meal she'd ever prepared. She was eternally grateful when Mrs. Swanson rescued her in her struggles to make gravy—and that only Jake saw the bag of gizzards she accidentally left inside the bird while it was cooking.

Before she cleared the table, Mandy took a moment to sit back and look around her. How had this happened?

A year ago she'd rarely had a guest in this house. Now she'd just cooked Thanksgiving dinner for six people, and all of it had been edible. Okay, the temps had brought canned cranberry sauce and store-bought pie. But still.

"The sweet potatoes were amazing," Jake said. He sat at the end of the table across from Mandy. Like her, he seemed reluctant to move.

"It was my mom's recipe. The ingredients are really simple, but I've always loved it."

"Maybe next time I'll show you the family recipe for peppered baby carrots," Jake said.

Mandy slid an accusing stare his way. "You didn't tell me you could cook."

"You didn't ask." He winked across the table at her. "Remember, I'm the one who carved the turkey."

And that sounded a little like blackmail, because that was when he'd discovered the bag of giblets. Mandy glared at him, deeply content.

"Starting tomorrow, this house explodes," she said.

Jake lifted his eyebrows. "I thought that was what happened in your kitchen today."

She glanced toward the doorway that separated the dining room from the kitchen, loathe to think about the cleanup job that waited for her in there.

"She means the Christmas decorations," Mrs. Swanson said. "As I recall, that's a two-day project, isn't it?"

"Two and a half days if you count getting all the boxes put away again," Mandy admitted. She glanced at Jake, wondering how he'd react.

He said, "Need help with the lights outside?"

It was all so domestic that an errant thought winked into her mind. Starting the holiday season with Jake felt so natural, so right. She wondered, briefly, what it would be like to do it every year. But it was way too soon to think about a future with Jake. Wasn't it? Especially when his permanent home was on the other side of the country.

*Enjoy what you have,* she told herself. As she'd learned with her mother, you could never be sure how long you were going to have it.

She finished her glass of sparkling cider and stood. "I'll start coffee," she announced, "and if everybody can give me a hand clearing the table . . . by the time I'm done straightening the kitchen, I think we'll all be ready for pie."

# Chapter 17

*How did they do it?* Jake wondered.

The morning after Thanksgiving, the town of Tall Pine had turned into a holiday wonderland. Arches of Christmas lights stretched across Evergreen Lane from one side to the other, and the lamp posts were wrapped in pine garland and red velvet bows. The sidewalks were clustered with shoppers, and Phyllis's hotel was full to the seams.

The only thing missing was snow. Jake hadn't seen any since that night on Mandy's front porch. He'd never talked to anyone else in town who'd seen that snow, either.

It still wasn't dark yet by the time he went to pick up Mandy at the store at the end of the day. The arches of Christmas lights couldn't be seen to their full advantage, but they were turned on anyway. Inside the store, he found Mandy and Mrs. Swanson coaching two of the teen holiday workers as they straightened the chaos of the store shelves.

Mandy was flushed, as if she'd just come in from a snowstorm. Obviously it had been a busy day. But unlike the fatigue she'd shown the day of the sidewalk sale, tonight she seemed exhilarated. He noticed her earrings: round red Christmas ornaments.

She greeted him with a bright smile. "It's going to be a little longer tonight," she said. "There's a lot of straightening up to do for tomorrow, and the register might take a little longer."

"Busy day?" he said unnecessarily.

"And how." The store speakers were still playing as Andy Williams sang about the most wonderful time of the year. "The day after Thanksgiving is always insane. It'll calm down a little tomorrow. What did you do today?"

"Finished up on a proposal to make a Christmas hotel glow." He kissed the tip of her nose. "When you're done, let's get a bite, and I can help you with those decorations at your house."

A shadow crossed her face. "You can't see the house yet. To look upon it is to go mad."

He frowned. "When did you start?"

"After you left last night, and a little this morning. When you work at a store during Christmas, you've got to grab the time whenever you can."

"So where do we go?"

If it was possible, her smile got brighter. "I've got just the place."

Forty-five minutes later, Jake stood in a crowd of people singing Christmas songs in front of a big pine tree outside the town hall. He'd passed the tree a dozen times in his dealings with the council. He'd never realized it was *the* tall pine of Tall Pine.

Was it the tallest one in town? It was hard to tell. Secretly, he suspected it had been the tallest tree conveniently located when the town was being planned. But he wouldn't have dreamed of saying that out loud, especially not in front of the enthusiastic group curved around the tree now for Tall Pine's sixty-eighth annual Christmas tree lighting.

*"Let it snow! Let it snow! Let it snow!"*

Funny how many Christmas songs revolved around snow, especially in an area where snow was so sporadic. When he'd talked to his parents yesterday, they said they'd had an inch and a half last week. A mountain town that didn't get enough snow to support a ski resort must struggle to compete for its share of the tourist trade. A reminder to Jake that this hotel could really do some good.

He'd spent too much time in front of his laptop today, he thought, as Mandy's voice reached his ears:

*"Let it snow! Let it snow! Let it snow!"*

Her voice pulled Jake back to the scene unfolding around him, and he pushed his internal accountant to the back of his brain. This was the world Mandy loved, and she never got tired of it. And the tree wasn't even lit yet.

Ten minutes later, the town officials took turns giving speeches, mercifully short, before deeming it was time to turn on the lights of the tree. Winston Frazier himself led the countdown, sporting a wider smile than Jake had ever seen on the man.

When the tree lights came on, the results were so bright Jake had to squint for a moment after so long standing in the dimness. A collective "ahh" rose up from the crowd, and Jake found himself drawing in his breath. The blended glow of red, green, blue, orange and white lights washed over the crowd, and the scene became timeless. The coats, knit caps and scarves the people around him wore could easily have been seen at the town's first tree-lighting sixty-eight years ago. The tree even looked bigger.

Without any apparent prompting, the crowd started to sing "Silent Night."

Mandy's voice stood out to him above the others, not just because she was standing next to him, and not because her voice was better than anyone else's, although it did have a sweet timbre. Just because it was Mandy's.

Jake looked down at her, and the glow on her face was more than the soft, colored light cast by the tree. It was a look of pure joy and contentment. *She does this every year,* he thought. *And every year, she loves it just as much.*

Was it because she'd lived her entire life in the same town and didn't have anything to compare it to? If that were the case, you'd think the brightness in her eyes would have gotten dimmer by now. She'd stayed in Tall Pine, taken a ton of ribbing about her vision of Santa Claus, and still she glowed. Maybe that was because this was where she truly belonged. Maybe Mandy's roots in this town ran as deep as the roots of the Tall Pine tree.

Up to now, Jake reflected, he'd been content to move from place to place. It had been convenient, he supposed, to avoid any reminders of past mistakes, to start over again in a new place and make a fresh impression.

Maybe it was time for him to put down some roots, too.


After "Silent Night," the crowd dispersed. Most of them split off to choose between two rapidly forming lines: one for hot chocolate from a kiosk outside, the other to see Santa Claus in the gazebo at the heart of the town square. Mandy watched the line of children for Santa, holding their parents' hands or, unable to contain their energy, jumping up and down in excitement. The figure seated in the large chair at the top of the gazebo wore a bright red suit.

She thought of Kris Kringle's line in *Miracle on 34th Street:* "I am not in the habit of substituting for spurious Santa Clauses."

Mandy looked away. She knew there was no harm in it. After all, she'd been to see Santa—or one of his numerous "helpers"—in the department store several times before she was eight. She wondered if Jake had done it too, but decided not to ask. They'd hit some ticklish territory the night they talked about the Christmas hotel, and neither one of them had brought up Santa Claus since. They'd tacitly agreed to disagree, and for the moment it seemed best to leave it that way.

Maybe Jake had the same thought, because when she turned to him, his attention was on the line for hot chocolate, every bit as long as the Santa line.

"Looks pretty daunting," he said. "Want to get some dinner?"

"Sure."

Jake seemed quieter than usual as they walked to the car, fingers intertwined.

"What did you think?" she asked him. "Too corny?"

"I didn't think there was such a thing as 'too corny' with something like this." He squeezed her hand. "I thought it was great."

"I'm glad. I haven't missed it since I was thirteen, and I've been sorry about that year ever since."

"What happened when you were thirteen?"

She grinned. "What part of 'thirteen' don't you understand? I was in a bad mood about something. I don't even remember what. So we stayed home and had dinner, and I felt sorry for myself."

She tried to remember that year. Trying to redefine herself, be one of the cool kids, or at least to blend in. She hadn't even played much Christmas music that year. Almost as if she'd been trying to make herself as miserable as possible.

"Speaking of dinner," Jake said, "what sounds good to you?" They reached the truck, and he leaned against it, taking both of her hands in his. "Is there any place in town you've never been to?"

What a strange question. "Let me think." She didn't have to think long. "No."

"Come to think of it, I'm not sure there's any place *I* haven't been by now."

"Is that a bad thing?"

"No. In fact, it's kind of nice."

\* \* \*

It had to be the most nerve-wracking purchase of Jake's life.

Not just because he was standing at the counter of Tall Pine Jewelers, where a wide window offered anyone passing by a perfect view of the customer inside the store. Not just because he was buying something that represented a major lifetime decision.

As he stared down at the array of diamond rings in the glass case, it was the multitude of *little* decisions, the number of choices, that overwhelmed him. Which ring was the *right* ring? They sparkled in front of him on their bed of black velvet like so many stars in the night sky.

Once upon a time, not so long ago, he would have been practical and taken the girl with him to pick out the ring. But the girl was Mandy. Taking her shopping for her own engagement ring would be contrary to everything about her.

If he'd gone to an out-of-town jeweler to choose the ring, at least he could have been sure of keeping it a secret. But *that* ran contrary to everything Jake believed about loyalty and business ethics. He wanted to support the town he'd struggled, and eventually reached an understanding, with. He had to buy the ring in Tall Pine.

"See anything you like?" the woman behind the counter prompted him. Fortyish, a little heavyset, with a patient smile, she'd stood back quietly while Jake surveyed the rings for the last ten minutes. Or was it twenty? It felt like he'd been taking up the woman's time for hours.

Jake rested his elbow on the glass and leaned on his right hand, hoping the hand would obscure his face from any curious passersby.

White gold or yellow gold, round or square, marquis-shaped or pear-shaped . . . Jake stared into the case, bewildered and intimidated, trying to focus on one ring at a time. And then he knew.

"That one," he said, pointing.

It wouldn't beat most of the others for carat weight. But the diamond in the center had a circle of smaller diamonds clustered around it, giving the ring a warmth that shimmered. It reminded him, suitably enough, of a Christmas tree. Or fresh snow.

The clerk drew the ring out of the case with what looked like an approving nod. As Jake held the ring between his fingers, watching the sparkling stones wink their own approval at him, the most nerve-wracking question of all made his heart thump so hard he was sure the clerk could hear it.

He was gambling that Mandy would say yes.

He swallowed hard and did what his gut told him to. "I'll take it."

This time the approval in the woman's smile was

unmistakable. Nerve-wracked or not, Jake mustered a smile of his own.

"Now, I'm going to state the obvious," he said.

"What is that?"

"This *has* to be a secret. Remember, it's Christmas."


"You're sure you want me to open it now?" Mandy asked.

Jake had set the narrow, flat box on her knees. An early Christmas present, he said.

Mandy didn't believe in peeking at presents, and they really shouldn't be opened till Christmas. But once she had a present in her hands, with permission to open it, it was awfully hard to stick to the rules.

"It wouldn't do you much good by Christmas," he said.

She fingered the red and green foil wrapping, tied together with curling ribbon. He'd gone to some trouble to make the package enticing, and she had a feeling it held something major. Its shape and size suggested nothing so strongly as a necktie.

Mandy fingered the ribbons, letting the mystery drive her crazy a few seconds longer before she carefully slid the ribbon down the corner of the box and started peeling at the tape that held the wrapping paper.

"You're not one of those people who saves gift wrap, are you?" he asked.

"No. *That's* crazy. It's just so pretty—" She peeked up at him. "I like to make it last."

"Good thing I gave it to you a couple days early, then."

A piece of paper tore away with the tape, and Mandy gave in, tearing the paper.

Inside the box was a long white envelope. Mandy bit her lip and smiled at Jake again. "Now who's drawing things out?"

Mystified, she opened the envelope and stared at a plane ticket. To New York City. Dated December twenty-second. She looked up at him, confused.

"I've got one just like it," he said.

He rested his hands on her knees. "Remember, I told you I always go home for Christmas. This year I want you to come, too."

Her brain was having trouble firing. "But the ticket says New York."

"Did you know," he said, "that Scranton's only a couple of hours from New York by car? And there's a certain big tree at Rockefeller Center?"

Comprehension dawned. "Where Will Ferrell kisses Zooey Deschanel in *Elf.*"

He grinned. "I wasn't sure if you liked that movie or not. But I figured you'd love the tree. I've never been to see it myself, and I thought . . ." He shrugged.

"Thank you." A lump formed in her throat. "This is amazing."

Her mind raced. *Christmas at Jake's. Meeting his parents. Flying to New York.*

Then her heart dropped to her shoes. *The store. My job. Mrs. Swanson.*

"Jake, it'll be three days before Christmas. I don't know if Mrs. Swanson—"

Jake rested a hand on hers. "I thought of that. I talked to her. Gemma's on break from school by then, and Mrs. Swanson is sure she'd love the extra hours. Gemma's not *you,* but Mrs. Swanson is really happy with how well she's caught on."

"Me too." It stung a little, to think anyone could fill in for her job.

Jake was giving her that steady look she'd come to know so well. "Mrs. Swanson said if anyone ever deserved a Christmas vacation, it's you. So unless you'd really *rather* stay—"

"Oh, no. You've got to be kidding."

A grin broke out over Jake's face, chasing the serious look away.

# Chapter 18

December always swept Mandy up in a red and green whirlwind: decorating the tree, bagging merchandise, hearing Christmas music on the radio, trying to make the season last.

This year, the whirlwind spun twice as fast. She battled the clock, trying to finish needlepointing Jake's stocking in time for Christmas without his seeing it. She was pretty sure he'd like it. But hand-stitched or not, it seemed pretty small compared with a ticket to New York. *It's the thought that counts,* she reminded herself.

Then she bought a chocolate-brown knit pullover, the color of Jake's eyes, to supplement it.

The night before they left, they were about to settle in for a pizza at Mandy's house. Except she couldn't settle anywhere. She tried to run through a mental checklist of everything she didn't want to forget.

"Toothbrush, toothpaste . . ."

Jake grinned as he draped his jacket over the back of the couch. "You do know they have tooth-paste in Pennsylvania, right? If you forget some-thing it's not the end of the world."

"I know. Sorry. I'm just a little nervous."

"Just make sure you packed a few extra layers," Jake said. "I checked the weather report. It's cold out there."

The last phrase echoed in her head. Mandy caught herself humming, "Baby, It's Cold Outside" as she went to double-check her suitcase. These days, everything was a Christmas song cue, and they'd just heard the She and Him version of the song on the CD player in Jake's truck.

The song was still stuck in her head when Jake went into the kitchen to call for pizza.

The CD. She'd left it in the player in Jake's truck. The truck they'd be returning to the rental agency at the airport tomorrow. The way her mind was spinning, she was bound to leave it in there. She'd better grab the disc now before she forgot.

Mandy glanced at the table in the hallway for the keys to the truck. Not there. "Jake?"

"Just a sec," Jake called from the kitchen. "Their phone's ringing."

She spotted Jake's coat hanging over the back of the sofa. The keys were probably in there. She turned the coat and reached into one of the

**247**

pockets. Her fingers brushed over something hard, yet velvety. What could . . . ?

She traced the shape of it in her hand. A small, square, velvet box.

Her heart thrummed. She couldn't think of many things that came in small, square velvet boxes. Mandy tried to temper her racing thoughts with reality.

*A necklace,* she told herself. *It could be a necklace. It could even be a necklace for his mother.*

It was a pretty small square for that, though.

"Mandy?"

Alarm shot through her. She jerked her hand out of his pocket. But Jake wasn't there, and she realized his voice was still coming from the kitchen. She stepped back, putting as much distance between herself and the coat as she could before she answered. "What?"

"Was it mushrooms or olives you wanted on your half?"

She swallowed. "Mushrooms, please."

She backed farther away from the coat, feeling her face burn as fiercely as if she'd been caught stealing a fistful of candy from an orphan. In the next room, she heard Jake finish their pizza order. *Act naturally.* Whatever that meant.

Thoughts replayed in her mind: *Christmas at Jake's. Meeting his parents. Flying to New York.*

*To see that romantic tree.*

And suddenly, the only natural thing she could possibly do was plunk down on the couch before her knees buckled. She couldn't keep her heart from pounding, but if she worked at it, maybe she'd be able to breathe normally. If that box was what she thought it was, Jake had one more surprise in store on this trip.

A Christmas proposal. The thought sent a thrill through her. For the second time in her life, she found herself pinching herself on this couch.

A tiny voice inside wondered, *Am I ready for this?*

In the next room was a man as rational as she was fanciful. She knew she loved him. She also knew he'd never believe in something as illogical as Santa Claus.

Was this the right thing?

Jake walked in, a wry smile on his face. "You do know that vegetables on pizza are a sin against nature."

And her heart sang *yes*.

"What did you want a minute ago?" he asked.

"Oh." She closed her eyes and thought. She didn't want to mention anything about car keys or jacket pockets, nothing that would make him suspect she'd found the box. "I forgot." She opened her eyes. "My mind's a little muddled."

He sat beside her on the couch, and she resolutely ignored the sleeve of his jacket when it dropped to dangle behind him. "You've never been this far from home, have you?"

"No. And I've never flown before."

"Don't worry. You'll have plenty of time to get used to it. Airports are kind of a separate eternity." He paused. "One more thing you might want to bring along."

"What's that?"

"A copy of *War and Peace*."

It wasn't until the next morning that Jake remembered the airline regulations about the size of toiletries. That led to a reshuffling of Mandy's luggage in her front entryway in the wee hours of the morning. Sure enough, most of the bottles were full-size, and she'd had them in her carry-on bag.

"But that's the most basic stuff," she said. "I thought it would be smart to have it in a carry-on."

"Once upon a time, I'm sure that was true. But they want to make sure terrorists aren't smuggling some sort of—"

He saw her pale, and he immediately regretted using the word.

"Hey, relax. It's just a hassle. They do it to make the trip that much safer." He picked up her newly arranged bag and opened her front door. "And if anything happens to the baggage—"

He saw her brow crease. He wasn't helping.

"—I happen to know my parents have plenty of shampoo at the house."

"They do know I'm coming, right?"

She did have a lot of things to be nervous about. He set the bag down, mindful of the ticking minutes and their hour-long drive to the airport. He hadn't missed a flight yet, but this would be a bad time to start. He'd worked it out so they should be able to reach Rockefeller Center by eight or nine p.m. if they had something to eat first; he didn't want them arriving starved, exhausted, or rushed.

Maybe he should have figured in an extra day of travel. Too late now.

He drew a deep breath and took a moment of precious time to put his arms around Mandy. "Yes," he said. "They do know you're coming, and they'll love you. That's the last thing in the world you need to worry about."

He kissed her, taking a few more of those precious moments to do it right. It would take a heck of a kiss to drive away worries about formidable parents, plane crashes, lost luggage and terrorists. He did his best.

When they reached the security line, it was Jake's turn to panic. He hadn't thought about the metal detectors and the ring in his coat pocket. There was no way he was trusting that particular item to any piece of luggage, carry-on or not.

*People walk through these things with their jewelry all*

*the time,* he reminded himself. Then winced when they made him put his coat on the conveyor belt along with all the other items to be x-rayed.

He watched Mandy walk through ahead of him, grateful that she didn't set the metal detector off. That was the last thing she needed. By the time Jake walked through the device after her, he saw his jacket waiting at the end of the conveyor belt. No beeps, bells or alarms.

When he got to the other side, Jake scooped up his coat, still striving for nonchalance, and gave the pocket a surreptitious squeeze. The hard, square shape assured him that the box was still there.

Thank God they'd stay behind airport security lines from here, and he wouldn't have to do this again on their stopover in Dallas.

As they boarded the plane, Jake's insides were coiled tighter than a spring. Beside him, he could tell Mandy was still nervous too, but she wore it on the inside, nearly as quiet and subdued as she'd been on their first date. Somewhat to his dismay, she seemed to have taken his advice to heart. She hadn't brought *War and Peace,* but she did seem intent on the book she was reading. Although Jake noticed she hadn't turned a page in quite a while.

"What are you reading?"

"*The Cricket on the Hearth.* I started it once a couple of years ago, but I didn't finish it."

One of Dickens's less successful Christmas stories.

"I had to read that in high school. I think it was pretty sappy."

She raised her head from her book and turned to him. "You don't think that about *A Christmas Carol,* do you?"

Her blue eyes were fixed on him as if the answer to that question was very important.

"Of course not," he was relieved to say truthfully. "Are you kidding? We watched—what, three movie versions of it this month?"

A smile shone from her face, the first real one he'd seen in the past few hours. As if she were glad that was settled.

She returned to her attempts at reading, while Jake wished for his own copy of *War and Peace.* A plane flight really wasn't a place for conversation, anyway. The only talkative people you usually saw on a plane were the ones no one wanted to sit next to.

He noticed she still wasn't turning many pages. He probably wouldn't have been able to concentrate either, whether it was Dickens, Tolstoy, or the latest bestseller. Tonight seemed far away. He didn't have any specific reason to think she'd say no. But he couldn't be sure she'd say yes.

At last they landed in Dallas. Mandy made a beeline for the ladies' room; Jake headed toward the food court, where he could scout out the possibilities for lunch. Belatedly, he took his phone off Airplane mode. His in-box didn't have many e-mails—after all, it was three days before Christmas—but there was a voice mail from the home office.

"Jake? This is Mark. Give me a call."

That was eerily nonspecific. Jake was tempted not to return the call, but his spider-sense told him he'd better.

He dialed Mark, keeping an eye toward the restrooms. Airports were easy to get lost in.

"Hey, Mark. What's the word?"

"I met with the board. They all agreed that the holiday hotel idea shows a lot of initiative, but it's not a direction they're ready to go yet."

Jake heard a little more after that—blah blah, hotel image, blah blah, different business model . . .

He didn't need reasons. He broke in. "And so, the Tall Pine project—"

"—is scrapped. I'm sorry, Jake, but your track record speaks for itself. You're too valuable to use in an area that just isn't worth the hassle. I know it's a drag. You tried like hell on this one, but four months is long enough."

Across the airport lobby, Mandy emerged from the ladies' room. Momentarily disoriented, she turned in the wrong direction, looking for him.

Jake turned his back and found a pillar. It was a bad time to hide from Mandy. But at least it gave him something to lean against.

"Mark, are you serious?" The question was rhetorical, a reflex, like air rushing out of his lungs after a sucker punch.

"Sorry, buddy," he said. "The good news is, we've got another project lined up for you, and you don't have to start until after the first of the year. No one's going to be doing any business between now and then, anyway."

"Where is it?" *Somewhere in Southern California, please.*

"Pensacola Beach. It's beautiful out there. I envy you, working in Florida in January."

Florida. With Mandy in California and his family in Pennsylvania. Regal Hotels couldn't have picked a place on the continental U.S. farther from the two places that mattered to him most.

He'd gotten Tall Pine to say yes. He'd been worrying about Mandy's saying yes. Why had it never occurred to him that his own company might say no?

And of course, they were confident Jake would say yes. He'd spent the past five years jumping at a moment's notice, going wherever they sent him, thinking that was the road to success.

Maybe if he really talked to Mark, told him a little about his own plans . . .

But first, he had to hang up and find Mandy before she got lost.

"Jake?" Mark prompted. "Are you still there?"

"I'm at the airport now, Mark. I've got to run."

"That's right, you're heading home for the holidays, aren't you?" Mark couldn't have sounded more cheery.

"Yep. I'll talk to you later." Jake hung up.

He pocketed the phone and felt it thunk against the red velvet box. His heart sank. A ring in his pocket and no clear plan for the future. With Mark's piece of news, as of this moment, he wasn't even sure he was going to stay with Regal Hotels.

He stepped from behind the pillar, searching the crowd for Mandy. The first time he'd been to this airport he'd spent forever going in circles, trying to find his way out of the terminal for the wrong airline.

Usually, Mandy's red jacket would have been easy to spot. Now, three days before Christmas, the terminal was a veritable sea of festively dressed travelers in bright red and green. It could be like a needle in a haystack.

Then his eyes found her as surely as if a spotlight had been aimed at her—beautiful dark hair tumbling over the red wool on her shoulders, her gaze roaming slowly around her as she walked toward the food court.

His heart clutched. He couldn't lose her, literally or figuratively. He had to find a way to make this work.

"Mandy."

She swung around, her smile showing relief. "There you are. I wasn't sure I was in the right place."

"You did good. You almost beat me to the food court."

She studied him, a small crease forming between her eyebrows. "Are you okay?"

He worked up a smile that was mostly a grimace. "You just missed it," he said. "One of those baggage carts ran right over my foot."


The tree at Rockefeller Center was everything Mandy had imagined, only more so.

She had to crane her neck to look up at it. It towered over the square, its multicolored lights giving off a radiant shimmer. For a moment she closed her eyes, looking at the afterglow on her eyelids, trying to preserve the mental image of the tree in her mind.

But she was here, now, so she opened her eyes and took it in once again.

Forcing as much understatement as she could into her voice, she said, "Now, that's a tree."

Jake stood behind her and wrapped his arms around her, a plus in more ways than one because the cold at Rockefeller Center was also more than she'd ever imagined. They were far from the only people here, but the crowd was light enough that their fellow tourists receded to the background.

"About thirty thousand lights," he murmured in her ear, and this time it was the warm vibration of his voice that made her shiver. "Over seventy feet tall. That star at the top is nine and a half feet across."

She nodded. Leave it to Jake to learn all the facts and figures. But she'd done her homework too. "It takes a custom trailer to get it in here."

"And every year in January, they recycle the tree for lumber or mulch."

"Jake!"

"What? Oh, I'm sorry. I forgot. Don't say 'mulch' in front of the tree."

Mandy leaned into him, relishing the moment. Jake had been subdued the past several hours, but then, she probably hadn't been a ball of fire herself. A long day of travel could do that to anyone. She told herself that was what spending your life with someone was like. Being together for the tedious stuff, the boring stuff, even the hard stuff. They'd had a little practice so far. But hopefully, there was a lot more to come.

She waited, sure Jake could feel her heart pounding underneath his embrace. But something wasn't happening.

Jake took his eyes from the tree, burying his lips

in Mandy's hair. So much planning had gone into this moment, and it was nearly perfect.

Even with his arms around Mandy, he could practically feel the ring in his pocket, burning away like radium. He wanted to reach for it. He wanted to say what he'd come here to say, but something had him by the throat. *Plenty of people get married without a plan,* he thought. He just never thought he'd be one of them. Right now he was staring at a big fork in the road. One of the signs was pointing toward *Florida.* The other one was aimed at *Unemployment.*

He needed to offer her a better plan than that.

Turning her toward him, he cupped her face in his palms, trying to drink in every detail of her face under those lights. Trying to think of something to say that was worthy of the moment.

Words failing, he kissed her. It was sweet, delicious, and possibly their most tender kiss yet. Jake held on to her, making it last, because in that moment anything seemed possible.

Finally he looked down at her, and it was just him, Mandy, and the icy December air.

"I love you," he said, and never had the three words seemed so small and insufficient.

"I love you," she whispered.

A silence stretched out, until Mandy put her arms around his neck and held him tight.

*Say it anyway,* his mind whispered, but the words, and the moment, were gone.

# Chapter 19

Maybe the ring fell out of his pocket.

Mandy's eyes skimmed the sidewalk of Times Square for the ring—or the box—but it was hard because the pavement was jammed with passing feet, and the ring might be buried under piles of confetti anyway. The pop of hundreds of firecrackers rumbled under the noise of the bustling crowd. It was New Year's Eve; somehow she'd missed Christmas altogether, and where was Jake?

Back at Rockefeller Center, she realized. So how had she wound up at Times Square?

The rumble of the firecrackers got closer and more persistent, until it sounded like knocking.

"Mandy?" Jake's voice came to her, muffled, as if she were hearing him from underwater.

She opened her eyes. Daylight replaced the night lights of Time Square, and she found herself in a room she hazily recognized. She'd seen it for about five minutes last night when she and Jake had arrived at his parents' house. He'd led her, tiptoeing, up the stairs to the guest room at about one a.m. She remembered the comforter on the bed most, a dark blue plaid, fluffy with down.

Another soft knock came at the door across the room, and she tried to struggle the rest of the way up from muddled sleep. "Come in."

Jake opened the door, looking tidy and maddeningly refreshed. He paused just inside the doorway as he surveyed her in her horizontal, rumpled glory. Mandy pulled the fluffy comforter up to her chin and tried to assume a semi-sitting position.

"Sorry," he said. "But it's almost ten. I thought I'd better get you up and give you time to get started."

She brushed hair back from her face with one hand, holding on to the covers with the other. "That means it's—what—"

"Not quite seven in Tall Pine."

She rubbed her eyes, still trying to sort out the dream from the reality. So there wasn't an engagement ring lost under some ticker tape. Maybe there'd never been a ring at all. She looked at Jake as the fragments of last night started falling into place.

"You've got jet lag," he said. "It's normal. You've had a weird schedule, and your time zones are all messed up. But we've only got about two hours till the invasion."

Her brain was catching up. "All the aunts and uncles and cousins."

He nodded. "Right. And I wanted to give you time to meet my folks first, before we're up to our eyeballs in relatives."

His smile was sweet and just a little awkward. Maybe because she was in bed, clutching the comforter like a scared maiden. Truth be told, she didn't remember what she was wearing underneath.

"I'll get dressed," she said.

Jake nodded again and stepped back, his hand on the doorknob. "Right. The bathroom's next door. And my room's at the end of the hall"—he nodded to the left—"before the stairs. Come get me when you're ready."

When he closed the door, she lowered the covers and saw that she'd managed to pull on her jersey-style night shirt before she tumbled into bed.

Belatedly, her brain flashed a mental snapshot of what Jake had been wearing: a coffee-brown sweater she'd never seen before. Almost the same color as the one she'd bought him for Christmas.

As she got ready, she tried to sort through what had happened last night.

*So he didn't ask you to marry him. Big, fat hairy deal.* He'd planned this whole trip, brought her home to his family. And he'd told her *I love you* underneath the Rockefeller Center tree. What did she have to complain about?

But she couldn't shake the feeling that something had gone wrong.

When she went down the hall to find Jake, he was sitting at a laptop at a hutch-style computer desk. He swiveled quickly in his chair when she walked in.

"Ready?" He closed the lid on the laptop.

"Ready as I'll ever be." Meeting a boyfriend's parents. It was a ritual she only knew from the movies. He rose to lead the way out the door with hardly a glance in her direction.

"Jake?" Mandy didn't move to follow him yet.

He turned. "What?"

Was it her imagination, or did he seem preoccupied? "Do I look okay?"

She'd chosen a light blue sweater with a snowflake pattern, and her earrings were silver stars. She'd kept her hair and makeup simple. She hadn't wanted to take long, and it seemed best not to stray from the tried and true.

He didn't stop long to examine her, but his smile looked genuine. "You're perfect." He took her hand and kissed her lightly. "Let's go."

Still holding hands, they went down the stairs. The Wyndhams' two-story house reminded her of the classic American family home in just about every Christmas movie she'd ever seen, tidy and much more spacious than her house in Tall Pine. Family photos worked their way down the wall alongside the stairs, and pine garland wound around the banister. The effect was homey, but by the time they reached the bottom of the stairs, Mandy had time to conjure up a mental image of a forbidding New-England-style couple with stern countenances and—

A woman emerged from a room around the corner, and Mandy's vision dissolved like a soap bubble.

Jake's mother—she had to be Jake's mother—had short brown hair lightly spattered with gray, and a smile that reached all the way to her hazel eyes. She wore a black sweater decorated with an embroidered Christmas wreath.

"Good morning," she said. "You must be Mandy."

"And you're Mrs. Wyndham. I'm so glad to meet you."

"Pam."

Mandy blushed and felt Jake squeeze her hand.

"Come back to the kitchen," Mrs. Wyndham said, turning back in the direction she'd just come from. "You must be starving."

Jake gave Mandy's hand another squeeze and let go. She felt, briefly, like a boat set adrift. "I'll go find Dad while Mom helps you get some breakfast."

Mandy tugged at her sweater and followed Jake's mother. So far the water seemed fine.

As they walked through the kitchen past the stove, delicious smells greeted Mandy. She must have been half-asleep to miss them until now. The aroma of turkey blended with half a dozen other tantalizing scents she couldn't immediately put a name to. And something else Mandy latched on to immediately. Coffee. She prayed there was some left.

Past the kitchen area, a bay window cast light on an inviting breakfast nook, with bench seats and red-and-white-checkered seat cushions. "Have a seat," Mrs. Wyndham said. "Would you like some coffee?"

"I'd love it," Mandy confessed. "But really, that's all I need. You're in the middle of cooking for—"

"Don't worry about it. I didn't have to make anything for Jake this morning. He was already up when I got down here."

"You're kidding." Mandy sat on the checkered cushion.

"It's called long experience with air travel." Jake's voice preceded him into the room. "I'll probably crash around three."

She looked up to see Jake standing with a slightly shorter man. He looked like an age progression of Jake some thirty years later—the same keen brown eyes, the thick brown hair generously dusted with gray at the temples.

"Mandy, this is my dad," Jake said, prompting her to stand again and bump the table, which fortunately didn't have any coffee on it yet.

"Don't get up." The older man extended a hand to her. "Ben Wyndham. It's nice to meet you."

"Thanks. I mean, me too." Mandy decided to quit while she was ahead.

The men settled into the breakfast nook while Jake's mother poured coffee for all of them and brought Mandy a Danish for breakfast. Mandy glanced at the clock, saw it read ten minutes after eleven, and wondered how much time they had left before the relatives came crashing in.

With all of them seated, it suddenly felt like a summit meeting. Mandy clutched her coffee mug, grateful for the warmth, the caffeine, and something to hold on to. Determined not to clam up, she started with the most obvious statement she could think of: "You have a beautiful home."

Pam Wyndham nodded. "Thanks. We've been here nearly twenty years now. It's broken in."

Mandy nodded. "Jake tells me you—"

Jake's cell phone sounded. He pulled it out of his pocket and glanced at the screen. "Sorry. I need to take this."

And like a flash, the outer edge of the bench

beside Mandy was empty. For the second time this morning she felt unmoored.

Jake's father stared after him. "Do you have to put up with that a lot?"

"Actually, no." Mandy watched Jake's retreating sweater, trying not to feel deserted. "Maybe because the cell phone reception in Tall Pine is really iffy."

"What's Tall Pine like?"

"Very mountainy." Mandy made a face at the awkward word, but they seemed to know what she meant. "We're about seven thousand feet up, and it always smells like pine trees. It's pretty small, but it's nice."

"It sounds like an unusual choice for a chain hotel." That was Jake's father again. Weighing the pros and cons. She shouldn't be surprised.

"That's a problem Jake ran into." She wondered how much Jake had told them about Tall Pine, about her, about any of it. "It took a couple of months, but he got the town council to see the 'up' side of it."

Mrs. Wyndham broke in. "Jake tells me you work for a Christmas shop up there. That must be like working in a candy store."

"Or do you get tired of it?" his father asked.

Mandy nodded in Mrs. Wyndham's direction. "The first one."

\* \* \*

Jake finished his call and got back to the kitchen as quickly as he could. His folks were nice, but being left alone with anyone's parents right after meeting them would be a tall order for most people, regardless.

". . . and then Jake held up this bag of giblets," he heard Mandy saying. "I got the first bag out before I cooked the turkey, but I didn't know there was another one."

"So we threw away the evidence before anyone else saw it," Jake chimed in, sitting back down beside her.

"And he said, '*You saw nothing.*'" Mandy imitated his whisper as she glanced up at him, her eyes shining.

They spent the next fifteen minutes chatting until his mother got up to baste the turkey.

Mandy asked, "How can I help?"

Jake stood to free Mandy from the breakfast nook, and she sent him a smile as she went to join his mother. Those two were going to get along fine. He'd seen it as soon as they met. His dad was taking a more reserved role, but Jake knew better. Ben Wyndham just played things closer to the vest. And when you got down to it, this visit wasn't about getting their approval. Jake had brought her here, plain and simple, to show her off.

And, ideally, to welcome her into the family. Jake thought of the ring still waiting in his jacket upstairs, radiating like Kryptonite.

He excused himself from the table. The invasion would be starting any minute.


Mrs. Wyndham entrusted Mandy with some basic jobs of chopping and rinsing. She wasn't sure how necessary her help was, but as long as she wasn't getting in the way, she didn't care. Being here in this kitchen brought back memories of working with her own mother.

Gradually, the room started to flood with other females.

"I brought the green bean casserole. Where do you want it?"

"Here's the veggie tray. Want me to set it out in the living room?"

"Where can we stash the cake pops so the kids don't get to them before they eat?"

The rush of names made her dizzy. Anne and Liz were Pam's sisters. Marilyn was Anne's daughter, which made her Jake's cousin. Meanwhile, the rest of the house was filling with men and children as well. Mandy started wishing for a diagram. Introductions were made, and names started flying out of her head.

But she had a feeling they'd remember hers.

"So you're Jake's girlfriend!" an effusive brunette exclaimed. It sounded like big news.

"And you're . . . I'm sorry. Roberta?"

"Right." Roberta squeezed her arm. She had striking brown eyes. She had to be from Ben's side of the family. "I'm Jake's cousin. And your boyfriend was a *brat* to me when we were kids. He—"

"Get away from that one." She felt Jake's arms grab her by the waist from behind. "She lies."

"*You* lie! You broke that horse statuette and blamed it on me—"

Jake was literally dragging Mandy backward. "I told you. Lies, lies."

Mandy pulled away. "Wait. I think I'd better hear more—"

And he dragged her from the room. Into a closet. Where he kissed her until she could barely breathe.

"Jake!" Her giggle was muffled by the coats.

"Having a good time?" He rested his forehead on top of her head. In the light from the cracked-open closet door, she couldn't read his expression, but his voice sounded serious.

"I am. I just can't keep track of everybody."

"Don't try." He pressed a kiss to her forehead. "I know the adults, but I've known them all my life. I still have trouble with the kids, because they grow every year. And most of them will be gone by bedtime."

He opened the door and slipped out. Mandy emerged behind him, smoothing her hair. It didn't look as though anyone had seen them.

Mandy rejoined the kitchen crew as they laid the food out on a long table in the formal dining room. Before the meal started, a blond woman arrived with a light-haired, brown-eyed girl who barreled through the crowd straight to Jake.

"Uncle Jake!"

He lifted her in his arms, and the smile on his face was warm and bright. "Hey, Emmy."

So this was Emily. As Jake carried her back to her mother and set her down, Mandy saw she was wearing the pinecone necklace. Jake looked up, his eyes finding Mandy in the crowd. She hurried over for the introductions.

"Mandy, this is Susan, my brother's wife." He nodded at the pretty blonde. "And this is Emily. Emily, this is Mandy, the lady who sold me the necklace."

Emily smiled up at her. "Thank you."

"Don't thank me. Thank your Uncle Jake." Smiling, Mandy put her hands on her knees as she bent closer to Emily's level. "How old are you, sweetie?"

"Seven. I'll be eight in January. I'm in second grade."

"Really? I would have said you were a third-grader."

"People say I'm tall. My daddy's tall."

Mandy straightened, belatedly greeting the girl's mother. "Hi, Susan. It's nice to meet you."

Susan smiled, a hint of fatigue shadowing her eyes. "Nice to meet you, too. So you're here from California?"

Mandy nodded, stepping back when Jake's parents came through the crowd to greet the late arrivals. Pam Wyndham hugged Susan. "You're just in time for dinner."

"We would have been here sooner, but I had to work. I picked these up on the way." Apologetically, Susan held out a plastic grocery bag.

Ben Wyndham took the bag and peered inside. "Oh, you got the little red velvet cupcakes. Those are mine."

"Later," Mrs. Wyndham said firmly, and spirited the bag away to the kitchen.

"Susan's an RN," Jake murmured in her ear. "She works some really terrible hours. And my brother's deployed overseas. This is the first Christmas he hasn't been home."

Susan's faintly weary look made a lot of sense.

"Okay, everyone," Jake's father said, and Mandy was surprised how far his voice carried. "Time to pray for the meal."

Very few people were anywhere near the table, but she realized the dining table only would have held about half of them anyway. Everyone bowed his or her head where he or she stood or sat. Mandy tried to remember if she'd ever said grace as a family, and a lump formed in her throat. When the group said "Amen," she raised her eyes and turned to Jake.

And his cell phone went off. "Be right back," he said.

This time Mandy was literally adrift in a sea of people as they lined up for the table in a patient sort of disorder. Wait for Jake or help herself? Susan walked up to join her.

"It's not very formal," she said. "Everyone kind of grabs a seat where they can."

"You'd need at least two tables to do it any other way," Mandy said.

Emily quietly joined them as they worked their way toward the table. "Where's Uncle Jake?"

"His phone rang," Mandy said. "He'll be back."

She and Susan found a spot in the breakfast nook with Emily, one of the quieter places in the house. Mandy realized she'd spent the last hour and a half surrounded by a slowly building dull roar. The commotion was pleasant in its way, but the relative calm was a nice break.

While they ate, Emily regaled Mandy with questions about Tall Pine and the Christmas store. It was fifteen minutes before Jake rejoined them.

He seemed preoccupied. That seemed to be happening a lot today.

After the meal, Jake excused himself to make another phone call. He returned to find Mandy in the kitchen again, scraping plates and putting away food with Susan, Roberta and his Aunt Liz. Somehow they'd persuaded his mother she deserved a break and actually gotten her to take one. Emily sat in the breakfast nook, doing her best to absorb the girl talk. Jake took the opportunity to let the jet lag have its way and wandered into the living room to settle on the floor near the fireplace. His dad occupied his favorite spot in the armchair nearby.

Around them, relatives chattered. The fire was warm and relaxing. All was right with the world. Almost.

"You haven't asked me what I think."

Jake turned to regard his father lazily. "Do I need to?"

"No." His father smiled slowly. "She's terrific."

Propping himself up on his elbows, Jake closed his eyes, letting the heat of the fire soak into him.

"How bad is it?"

"What?"

Ben Wyndham regarded Jake with exaggerated patience. "Whatever's had you on and off the phone all day."

274

Jake sighed. "It's the difference between whether I can stay with Mandy in Tall Pine, or get dragged off to Florida. The home office isn't being flexible about it."

"So take her to Florida."

He couldn't imagine asking Mandy to leave Tall Pine. "I need a better plan than that."

"You always had a plan. I remember you making lists before you even got out of high school."

Jake grinned weakly. "And I'm still a million bucks shy of being a millionaire."

*"Planes, Trains and Automobiles."*

"We watched it on Thanksgiving." Jake grinned. "When her boss didn't want to watch *Ghost*."

"You sound like a match made in heaven."

# Chapter 20

"Tell me again," Mandy asked. "Why don't you have Christmas dinner on Christmas Eve, or Christmas Day?"

"We used to," Mrs. Wyndham said. "But the families kept getting bigger, and everyone wanted to spend Christmas at home with their kids. So we made it a night earlier."

"Got it." Mandy smiled. "The night before the night before Christmas."

Wedged between Mandy and Susan in the breakfast nook, Emily giggled. "Or Christmas Eve Eve."

"Christmas Eve Eve." Mandy nodded approval. "I like that."

"We'll be here for both nights this year," Susan said. "Ready to stay in your daddy's old bedroom with me tonight?"

It was early evening, and the hubbub was starting to die down as people settled around the house with cups of coffee or hot chocolate. Jake was on the phone, or e-mailing, somewhere. How much business was there to do two days before Christmas?

Emily said, "Last year I stayed in the guest room."

"Yes, because Daddy and I were both in his old room," Susan said patiently. "This year Mandy's in the guest room."

"Could I stay in the guest room with Mandy tonight?"

Susan chuckled. "The way you kick and thrash around, I think Mandy would end up on the floor."

Mandy grinned. It sounded as if Susan had helped her dodge a bullet, but Emily's request touched her. "Anyway, we're still next-door neighbors."

"I've thought about getting a different comforter for that guest room," Jake's mother said. "The blue plaid . . ."

The conversation went on, inconsequential and homey. The voices around her receded to a low hum. Mandy felt her head bob forward and snapped it up.

Emily giggled again. "Mandy's falling asleep."

She glanced at the kitchen clock. "That's pretty sad. It's only three o'clock back home."

"Flying does that to you," Mrs. Wyndham said. "I've seen Jake fall asleep at the dinner table."

Maybe that was what had happened to him this time. He could have collapsed in a heap on a couch or chair in some other room.

"You're welcome to lie down if you want to," Mrs. Wyndham said. "I should warn you, when Jake shows up again, he's likely to get up a vicious card game."

Mandy frowned. "For this many people?"

"Well, not everybody plays. But I've seen us get nine or ten people around the dining table for a game of Hearts. Or Pit."

"Pit?"

"It's loud and obnoxious," Roberta said. "It'll keep you awake for sure."

Beside her, Mandy felt Emily shifting as she swung her leg back and forth under the bench seat. She'd been sitting still for a long time, trying to blend with the adult women. As far as Mandy could discern, there were about half a dozen cousins spread around the house, but the closest to Emily's age was about ten. Some were in their early teens. Emily was the odd one out.

"You know what?" Mandy said. "I haven't gotten a good look at the Christmas tree yet. You want to show it to me, Emily?"

The girl was on her feet in a flash.

The Wyndhams' tree was on display in a bay window at the front of the house. The lights had been turned off when Jake and Mandy got in last night, but now its large multicolored bulbs shone warmly. An impressive number of packages were clustered under the tree, but it was the ornaments that captivated Mandy. Some of them had the look of pieces that had been around for a couple of generations: old-fashioned toy soldiers, candy canes and red hearts with some of their paint worn away. And she recognized several of the keepsake ornaments they'd carried at The North Pole over the years.

"We sold this one at my store a few years ago," she told Emily, pointing at a reindeer carrying a Christmas tree. "And this one." It was one of the eleven pipers piping, part of a "Twelve Days of Christmas" series.

"This one's my favorite." Emily pointed to a blown-glass Santa Claus.

"That is a nice one," Mandy agreed.

She studied Emily's profile in the muted glow of the Christmas lights. Her eyes were round, and Mandy guessed she was still a believer. Why did anyone have to grow out of it?

An oddly shaped red felt ornament with a few glued-on sequins caught her eye. Homemade, obviously. Mandy tried to decide if it was meant to be a stocking or a heart. She chose her words with care, in case Emily had made it. "What's this one?"

"A family argument." Jake's voice resonated behind them, startling Mandy and at the same time sending a warmth to her toes. She could tell from the way he sounded that he was *here* this time—not just in the room. His voice didn't have that preoccupied, half-present tone she'd heard so often today.

"My brother Tony swears that I made it," Jake went on. "I say it was him. Ugliest thing I've ever seen."

"But what's it supposed to be?"

"Until the artist claims ownership, I guess we'll never know." He kissed the top of her head.

"What've you been up to?" She tried to make her tone casual.

"Looking for people to play cards with. Are you game?"

"Sure, if you don't mind teaching me. My mom and I used to play gin, but that's more of a two-person game." She took Emily's hand. "And first, I think I need some hot chocolate to keep me going. Do you want a cup?"

Emily nodded eagerly, and they all headed for the kitchen.

"Jake's losing his touch," Roberta gloated as she won another hand.

"I'm taking pity on you," Jake returned, but it sounded like a stock answer.

Mandy watched as he picked up the next hand

and fanned out his cards. His studious frown said he was concentrating on something, but it didn't seem to be the game.

Not that she knew enough about the game to judge. Mandy had barely started to catch on to the eccentric rules of Hearts. The idea was to accumulate as few points as possible, and to avoid having hearts in your hand, unless of course you decided to go for *all* the hearts. The competition around the table was fierce, but the outcome clearly wasn't as important as the trash-talking.

"Besides," Jake said, scowling at his cards, "somebody needs to deal me a decent hand." He directed a glare across the table at the dealer, his Aunt Anne.

"I hear excuses," a cousin—was it Mike?—said.

*"And,"* Jake went on, as if to drown him out, "my good luck charm deserted me."

He directed a glance across the table, and this time the glimmer in his eye looked genuine.

Emily had pulled up a chair to sandwich herself between her mother and Mandy again, kibitzing on both of their hands. "I'm rooting for the girls," she said.

"Can't argue with that," Susan said.

"Traitor," Jake said.

While Jake made himself the target of the competing cousins, uncles and aunts, the one who was quietly making a killing was Jake's father. At the end of each hand they played, Ben Wyndham's score tended to be the lowest, when he was caught with any points at all. This older version of Jake fascinated Mandy, though she still wasn't sure what he thought of her. Both men had that keen, assessing way of looking at things, but Jake was much easier to read.

She'd thought so, anyway. The image she'd had of Jake kept shifting in and out of focus. She reminded herself again not to read too much into it. This was an entirely different setting, with a crowd of people and a lot of distractions. But he seemed strangely preoccupied, even around his own family.

The preteens had gotten hold of a video game system, and occasional roars came from the living room a few feet away.

When Emily started leaning on her mother's shoulder, Susan put an arm around her. "I think it's time to get you to bed," she said.

Emily surprised Mandy by giving her the first good-night hug when she made the rounds of the table before Susan took her upstairs to tuck her in.

Before the next hand could start, Mandy got up to freshen her hot chocolate. Learning her way around Pam Wyndham's kitchen hadn't taken long. More to the point, she felt welcome to do it. She started to reach for another instant cocoa packet from the basket on the counter, changed her mind, and poured a cup of coffee from the waiting carafe instead.

"Go easy on that," Jake said. "You don't want to bounce off the walls when it's time to go to sleep."

"I don't think that's possible."

"You'd be surprised at the tricks your system can play on you." He watched her as she poured. "I take it you're not ready to surrender on cards yet."

"Nope." She stirred in cream and sugar. "I'm not as bloodthirsty as the rest of you yet, but wait till I get the hang of it."

It was amateur trash talk, and it didn't sound convincing to her own ears. She picked up her cup with both hands and took a cautious sip to sample it without looking at Jake.

*Is everything all right?* she wanted to ask. Maybe things wouldn't feel so strange if she hadn't run across a velvet box in his pocket, a box she apparently wasn't supposed to know about. All her qualms could be the result of some pocket lint and an overactive imagination.

"You'll make a great mom," he said.

She turned toward him. "I will?" Mandy's throat burned unexpectedly, and it wasn't from the coffee she'd just sampled.

He wore that serious look again, brown eyes searching, that look she could feel to the tips of her toes. It was the expression she'd seen at Rockefeller Center last night. "You're terrific with Emily," he said.

"She's really sweet."

"It's good for her having you here. Susan has so much on her plate. She's working full time, and this is the first time Emily hasn't had her dad home at Christmas."

"I know how that feels."

Jake didn't reply. He brought a hand up to draw a slow line along the bottom of Mandy's jaw with one finger as he quietly studied her. She was aware of boisterous chatter from the next room, just a few steps away, but in here, the kitchen felt preternaturally quiet. Like the eye of the hurricane.

Mandy held his gaze, her heart thrumming.

Was this it? Right here, in the kitchen, with a cluster of relatives in the next room?

He kissed her. No mean feat, because she'd forgotten to set down her coffee cup. And she didn't dare try to set it down now, because the kiss was so soft, so slow, so thorough, she had no idea where the counter was. All she could do was close her eyes, try to remember she was holding a cup, and kiss him back with everything she had.

He drew away slowly. Mandy opened her eyes even more slowly.

Jake looked down at her, his eyes heavy, his voice husky. "We'd better get back to the battle."

\* \* \*

Somehow, after the card game, Jake found himself surrounded by a gaggle of females in the breakfast nook. Beside him, Mandy held yet another cup of coffee, her other hand holding his under the table.

He didn't bother to tell her that when he brewed the last pot of coffee, he'd switched to decaf when she wasn't looking. If she wasn't careful she'd be staring at the walls all night. He should have made her a pamphlet, *Jake's Guide to Jet Lag*. Although so far, she'd shown a high tolerance for caffeine. Even now, her eyelids looked heavy.

She sipped from her cup. "Sorry, Jake. You don't make coffee as well as your mother does."

He smirked, but didn't come clean.

Across from them sat his mother, Susan and his Aunt Liz. His father had retired to the living room to sit in the armchair and pretend to harrumph at the kids still playing video games on the floor. Jake knew better. Bet a poker match between his dad and Winston Frazier would be a sight to behold.

"Is anyone going to cut those kids off the video games?" Susan asked.

"Their parents will be collecting them soon enough," Jake's mother said.

The table settled into a contented silence, the

kind that came after a day of frenetic activity and too much food.

"This is my favorite place in the house," Mandy said.

Eyes turned toward her, and she looked self-conscious.

"I know what you mean," Jake's mother said. "The kitchen table is always kind of a magnet for the women. And the men usually settle in the living room."

This time eyes went toward Jake, who shrugged.

A moment later Mandy's head bobbed against his shoulder. She quickly jerked upright, finding the attention on her again. "I am *such* a wimp," she admitted. "I'm sorry. I'd better go to bed."

Jake, who was running on four hours of sleep, stood to let her out of the breakfast nook. He should walk her upstairs to her room, but if they were alone he was afraid he'd say too much, the way he almost had earlier tonight in the kitchen.

He caught her hand as she started to turn away. "Tomorrow will be quieter. I promise."

"I loved it," Mandy said with a smile that managed to include everyone at the table.

Silent approval followed her out of the room, leaving the air open for nosy questions. Jake was pretty sure his mom would know better, and probably Susan—

"Is it serious?" That would be Liz, who'd never

had children and therefore had no reason to read the Tact and Discretion section of the parenting manual.

"No, she's just some chick I met at the airport." Jake held a deadpan look, biting the insides of his mouth. He was rewarded with an uncertain blink from Liz before the other two women snickered.

"She's wonderful, Jake." And *that* was his mother, giving what sounded dangerously close to an endorsement, which he thought was also forbidden in the rule book.

"She put up with the hoard really well," Susan said.

"She enjoyed it." He didn't elaborate on Mandy's own lack of family. He knew by now how much Mandy hated the idea of being looked at as some kind of poor orphan. "She loves your girl."

"It's a good thing, because Mandy couldn't have gotten away from her if she tried. Usually you're the one she won't leave alone." Susan rested her head on the high wooden back of the breakfast nook's bench seat. Jake saw faint smudges of fatigue under her eyes that even skillful makeup couldn't cover. She'd always been pretty, and she still was, but she didn't have Mandy's magic. Then again, who did?

"I'm surprised you're not asleep yet," Jake said.

"I'm headed there pretty quick," she said.

"When's the last time Tony got through to you on the phone?"

"It's been about a week. Everything's fine there, but his hours are so strange, and communication is so spotty. He says they promised him this is his last time going overseas. It's been hard on Emily this year, especially having him gone for Christmas. And then there's the Santa thing."

Jake snapped to attention.

His mother said, "Are the kids at school being skeptics?"

"Yep. Second grade, and a lot of them are saying there's no Santa Claus. She hasn't come right out and asked me, so I haven't said anything."

Jake took a swig from Mandy's abandoned, half-empty coffee cup and winced at all the cream and sugar.

"That's another reason to wish Tony were here," Susan was saying. "I'd rather have him here to deal with it." She ran a hand through the fringe of bangs on her forehead. "He's the one who's made it so convincing. Leaving footprints in front of the fireplace, shaking sleigh bells outside . . ."

And Tony was the one who'd killed Santa for Jake. "I can shake some bells tomorrow night," he offered. But was it the right thing to do?

She smiled wearily. "Can you drag them on the

top of the roof to make it sound like reindeer hooves?"

His brother did *that*? He smiled wryly. "Not in a two-story house, I can't."

"I just don't know what I'm going to tell her if she asks me point-blank, and I'm afraid it's coming."

*The truth,* Jake would have said a few months ago. Now he wasn't so sure.

# Chapter 21

Mandy woke once again to bright sunlight and sat upright in bed. How much of the day had she slept through this time?

The display on her cell phone said it was nearly nine o'clock. Six a.m. at home. She dressed as quickly as she could. This time she wore her favorite holiday sweater: a no-holds-barred Christmas tree made of beads and sequins on a black background. After all, it was the day before Christmas.

The house seemed unusually quiet after yesterday's frenzy. She peeked in the open door of Jake's bedroom. No one there, although the open lid of his laptop hinted at recent activity.

Downstairs, she found him in the kitchen, toasting an English muffin. "Where is everybody?"

Jake ticked on his fingers. "My mom and dad, last-minute shopping. Emily, probably shaking presents under the tree. And Susan, unfortunately, getting ready for work. They called her in this morning."

"On Christmas Eve?"

"I know. But it *is* a hospital."

Jake had vanished again by the time Susan came down the stairs wearing a warm, furry coat over her uniform. Emily, sitting under the tree, viewed her unhappily. "I wish you didn't have to go."

"I know, honey." Susan bent to kiss Emily's forehead. "But I'll be home before Santa comes."

Mandy saw a frown wrinkle Emily's brow as her mother kissed it. And when Susan left, the house was quieter still.

*All is calm . . . all is bright.*

Too calm, Mandy decided. And with Jake upstairs, working on his laptop, it was likely to stay that way. For a seven-year-old, it was always a long wait until Christmas morning.

"A little boring after yesterday, isn't it?" Mandy asked.

Emily nodded, looking downright mournful as she contemplated the tree.

"I have an idea," Mandy said. "Do you usually put out cookies and milk for Santa Claus on Christmas Eve?"

The little girl nodded again, but her solemn expression didn't lift.

"Well, it looks like we have some time to kill today," Mandy said. "How about if you and I bake some homemade cookies for Santa?"

This time Emily's nod was vigorous.

"Come on. Let's see if we have what we need in the kitchen. If we don't, we'll go to the grocery store."

Mandy took inventory in Pam Wyndham's kitchen, hoping she wasn't being too presumptuous. Flour and sugar, check. Butter and eggs, check. Vanilla, baking soda, salt . . .

"Now, where do you suppose your grandma would keep chocolate chips?"

Emily rummaged through the pantry and produced a bag of chips.

"Eureka!" Mandy winced inwardly. Her cheer sounded forced to her own ears. But it got a smile out of Emily, and those were harder to come by today. The seven-year-old was such a sweet combination of silly and serious, it tugged at Mandy's heart.

Jake emerged from down the hall.

"Hi," Mandy said. This time she didn't bother asking where he'd been. His behavior since they got here had been inconsistent, to say the least, but she wasn't going to worry about mixed signals now. It was the day before Christmas, and there was baking to do. "Do you think your mom's going to mind my raiding her kitchen to make cookies?"

"For cookies? I don't think you'll get any complaints around here."

"They're for Santa," Emily chimed in.

Jake's brow furrowed as his eyes went from Emily to Mandy. She had a feeling he was trying to say something with that look, but it was hard to interpret, especially with Emily starting to bounce impatiently on her toes.

"What do we do first?" Emily prodded.

"Well—" Mandy turned to face the girl. "Have you ever made cookies?"

"I've helped before."

"Okay. Then you know it can get messy. That's a pretty sweater you're wearing. Do you know if your grandma has an apron anywhere?"

Emily frowned, trying to think.

Jake nodded at the china hutch across the room. "Top drawer, I think. Although I'm not sure how I even know that."

"Maybe you made cookies for Santa before," Emily said.

"If I did, I did *not* wear an apron." Jake's eyes followed his niece as she skipped to the cabinet. His frown lingered faintly.

Emily pulled open the drawer. "I only see one."

"That's okay." Mandy glanced down at her sequined sweater. "I'll find a sweatshirt upstairs to change into."

Jake followed her upstairs to the guest room and closed the door behind them.

Mandy looked at him quizzically. "Um, you're not helping me change."

He leaned back on the door, grasping the knob awkwardly. "I know. I wanted to talk to you for a minute."

Mandy thought of the Rockefeller Center tree. Of last night in the kitchen. But this didn't look like good news. She eyed him cautiously. "Okay."

"Emily's been asking—questions. About Santa." He paused. "And if it comes up today—well, I was wondering what you'd say."

*Oh, no. Not this. Not now.*

Mandy's mouth went dry. "What do you want me to say?"

"I'm not sure." Jake avoided her eyes, and that wasn't like him. "Susan's been trying to figure out how to handle it, too. I just thought we should get on the same page. And not say anything too—fanciful."

The room got very, very quiet. So quiet that Mandy imagined she could hear Emily downstairs, rummaging for bowls and spoons. She knew full well the sound couldn't travel through that door and up the stairs, any more than Jake's niece could hear their voices. But Mandy also knew she didn't want Emily overhearing any of this.

Mandy spoke in a whisper. "Childhood is short enough as it is. It's the only time most people really believe in Santa. Why take that away?"

"I wouldn't want to." Jake stepped closer to Mandy as he lowered his voice to a near-whisper.

"But I think maybe . . . by the time they ask, they're ready to know the truth."

That last word made her wince. "Your truth is a little different from mine."

"I know." Jake studied her, and she knew he was trying to be careful. Trying, diplomatically, not to offend her. "But an eyewitness account, at this point . . . it might do more harm than good."

Mandy stared at him, her heart sinking. "I don't get it. When you heard me tell the story to kids in Tall Pine, you thought it was adorable."

"I guess it's because those kids—I don't think they were really questioning yet."

"Or maybe it's because they weren't related to you." She fought the feeling of hurt rising into her throat. "That's it, isn't it? You're afraid I'm going to warp your niece?"

"That's not what I said," Jake stammered. "I was just afraid you might—get caught off guard. This is a rough year for her, and—"

"You think I don't know that?"

"—and I don't want to set her up for disappointment."

It was all she could do to hold her voice to a whisper. "So you want me to tell a seven-year-old girl there's no Santa Claus."

"I didn't say that! But let's just say, not every kid has the experience you had."

Mandy took a deep breath. And another. She

still couldn't imagine what Jake expected her to say, but whatever it was, it was impossible.

"Why did you bring me here?" she said. "I can't see this your way. I can't. And I really can't stand the fact that you're never going to believe in me."

She couldn't see Jake. Her eyes were blurred over. But she couldn't think of anything else to say, either. So she brushed past him, out of the room, and started down the hall for the stairs. She'd only gotten a few steps when she felt Jake grasp her by the arms and turn her around.

"You know how much I don't believe in you?" He kept his voice low. "I've spent the last twenty-four hours on the phone trying to work out a small business loan so I can open your Christmas hotel in Tall Pine."

"But Regal—"

"—scrapped it. They want to send me to Florida. And I didn't want to leave Tall Pine. Or you. If that doesn't tell you anything . . ." He dropped his hands. "Then maybe you want too much."

He strode down the hallway, away from her.

Mandy tried to find her voice. "Jake?"

Emily called from downstairs. "Mandy?"

The door to Jake's bedroom closed quietly, and somehow that was worse than a slam.

Mandy dabbed at her eyes and hurried back down to the kitchen.

Emily stood waiting, a too-big green apron awkwardly tied around her. The cookie ingredients, bowls and measuring spoons were laid out on the kitchen island in an orderly fashion.

"You didn't change your sweater," Emily said.

"I forgot to pack my baking sweatshirt. Wasn't that dumb?"


All right, *that* went well.

Jake leaned back in the swivel chair in front of his laptop and closed his eyes. His muscles felt tight. He tried counting to ten. Then to twenty. Eventually he made it to a hundred and seventy.

This had to happen sooner or later, he thought. If things worked out the way he'd planned, they would have to go through this argument eventually, about their own child. Maybe it was best to have it happen now.

But what was the answer? He didn't see a lot of room for compromise.

When he opened his eyes, the laptop screen stared back at him like a vacant gray-black eyeball. He closed the lid. He wasn't going to hear back from anyone the day before Christmas, anyway.

What a great way to blurt out his half-baked plans for a future with Mandy. He had no idea where the two of them stood right now. There had to be a way to work this out. But at the moment, it felt as if he and Mandy were poles apart.

North Pole and South Pole.

Who was right and who was wrong was beside the point. Except that Emily was downstairs right now, and she could be asking for an answer any minute.

It was a good thing Mandy knew her cookie recipe by heart, because her mind was elsewhere.

It was an even better thing that she remembered to double-check the recipe on the bag of chocolate chips, because in Tall Pine, she always used the high-altitude instructions.

"Less flour, more sugar," she murmured, while Emily looked on with concern.

Her hands shook as she fished the excess flour from the bowl they'd just poured it into, taking care not to disturb the baking soda and salt. Adding extra sugar to the other mixing bowl was easier. It was just a good thing she'd caught her mistake before they combined the two bowls.

"Disaster averted," she told Emily with a smile.

If only other things were as easy to fix. The argument with Jake kept echoing in her mind, and she hadn't had a chance to fully digest his news about the hotel. Suddenly his behavior made a whole lot more sense. Who else in the world would try to finance a hotel project two days before Christmas?

*You know how much I don't believe in you?* he'd asked.

Mandy bit her lip as she stared into the bowl of flour. Maybe she was the one who hadn't believed enough in *him.*

But that didn't solve the situation with Emily.

She turned her attention to her small baking partner, who'd worked so meticulously alongside her to get the measurements right. "Now we stir it all together," Mandy said.

"Shouldn't we put in the chocolate chips first?"

"No, first we mix everything else. The chips come last. Don't worry. I don't think there's a chance either of us will forget those."

Mandy combined the two mixtures into the larger bowl, blending them just enough so that the flour wouldn't fly everywhere. Then she pushed the bowl in front of Emily. "Now it's your turn to stir," she said. "I warn you, it takes muscle."

It would take time, too, but that was something they definitely had. It wasn't even noon yet.

Emily set fiercely to work, golden brown bangs falling over her forehead, her tongue between her lips in concentration.

Mandy asked, "Do you usually put cookies out for Santa at home?"

Emily nodded, her head still bent to her work. "And my dad goes outside to check for Santa with binoculars. When he sees the lights from the sleigh, that's how he knows it's time for me to go to bed."

Mandy grinned. This, from the brother who'd told Jake there was no Santa Claus. "That's a good idea. I never thought of that."

Then Emily looked up, brown eyes shining like glass. "I miss my dad."

Mandy's heart wrenched. "And he misses you, too. You can be awfully proud of him. He's working hard for his country, but I know he's thinking about you and your mom."

Emily returned to her stirring with even fiercer concentration. Mandy tried to think of something to say that would help.

*At least he's stationed in a safe place, where there isn't any combat. . . .*

*And he didn't leave you because he wanted to.*

Then she thought of something better to say.

"Know what? We'll have to check with your mom, but I'm pretty sure we could send your dad a package with some of these cookies in it."

Emily raised her head again, and this time she smiled.

\* \* \*

Twenty minutes later, as Mandy spooned the first batch of cookies onto the baking sheet, Emily asked the familiar question.

"Is Santa Claus real?"

Mandy let a spoonful of cookie dough plop onto the metal sheet as her mind scrambled for an answer. "If he isn't, then who are we making these cookies for?"

*Plop.*

"Some kids at school say the moms and dads eat the cookies."

*Plop.*

"Some kids at my school used to say that, too." Mandy's eyes cast desperately around the room. How was she supposed to handle this?

*Plop.*

"But is it true?"

Jake walked in. As if he'd been in the next room all along. Mandy sagged with relief.

"Uncle Jake can answer that better than I can." She shoved the cookies into the oven, even though there was room for at least three more on the sheet. "I'll be right back. I've got to get this flour off me."

She rushed upstairs without meeting Jake's eyes. She'd left him holding the bag, but if he didn't want her messing things up, this was the way it had to be. Let him make the decision.

She pulled on a fresh sweater, not that the first one had really gotten any flour on it. But it gave her something to do as she tried to imagine what Jake would say.

Which part of Jake would win out—the one who'd smiled at her and called her the Christmas girl? Or the practical, "realistic" Jake, with his column of facts and figures and some blunt, disillusioning answer?

*Jake's nicer than that. This is the guy who's been sticking his neck out trying to build a whole hotel so he can stay with you. If he hasn't changed his mind by now.*


Jake sat on the sofa with Emily and thought, *So this is how it feels to hold someone's faith in your hands.*

He looked down into a pair of brown eyes so much like his own, so much like his brother's, and knew a simple black-and-white answer wouldn't do.

There were more important things to believe in than Santa Claus, to be sure. But at the moment, it sure seemed like he represented a whole lot. And after all the hemming and hawing, Jake knew he'd better come up with something good.

No way was he going to break his niece's heart. She deserved something more than a flat *no*.

"The fact is," he said slowly, "a lot of people do

stop believing in Santa Claus when they get older. It's the really lucky ones who keep believing."

Her eyes were fixed on him, and he was fumbling in the dark.

"You see, the same way those guys you see at the store are Santa's helpers? I think these days we're kind of Santa's helpers to each other." Jake nodded at the tree, the floor around it already laden with multicolored packages. "Not everybody needs another present. I don't think he could fit much more under there anyway, do you?"

Emily shook her head. The aroma of baking cookies wafted into the room, reminding him that a certain time limit was in play here.

"I think how real Santa Claus is depends on how much you believe in him," Jake said. "I'm not sure if he's a person like you and me, but he's the spirit of Christmas, and in that way, he's very real."

"So is he coming tonight?" Like any reasonable seven-year-old, Emily pressed for something tangible.

"Oh, he'll be here, all right," Jake said. "I'll admit, I've never seen him myself. But I kn—I've heard of people who have."

"Really?" Emily asked, clearly intrigued by the possibility.

"Really."

\* \* \*

When Jake went back upstairs to the guest room, the door was open. Mandy stood at the dresser brushing her hair, and he was pretty sure she wasn't really seeing her reflection.

"You win," he confessed, and she turned.

"I couldn't do it," he said. "Better get back down there, or your cookies are going to burn."

She looked at him, a world of questions in her eyes. But Emily and the cookies won out. She hurried past him down the stairs.

Jake followed a few minutes later and paused just outside the kitchen doorway. Silently, he surveyed the scene across the room.

Mandy was carefully moving the cookies from the hot baking sheet to a strip of wax paper on the kitchen island while Emily watched intently, her elbows propped on the edge of the countertop. As they stood over the cookies, heads close together, he saw a bond between them that felt almost conspiratorial. Something as timeless as Christmas itself.

"We'll let these cool for a couple minutes," Mandy told Emily. "But you *have* to eat at least one while the chips are still melty."

"Too bad the cookies won't be warm when Santa gets here," Emily said.

A smile came over Mandy's face, one that Jake knew well. That soft Christmas smile he'd seen for the first time in the middle of August.

"I guess not," Mandy said. "But we can make sure Uncle Jake gets one."

She wasn't looking at him, hadn't even seen him standing there, but Jake felt the glow of that smile even from across the room. Watching her, he thought he might understand, at least a little.

If he were Santa Claus, this was exactly the kind of girl he'd appear to.

# Chapter 22

Dusk came, and with it, a heightened sense of anticipation. Christmas Eve had arrived.

Mandy hadn't been alone with Jake since their last conversation. Jake's parents had returned while she was still in the thick of baking cookies, and she didn't know if she was disappointed or relieved. She knew she needed to set things right, and she wasn't sure what to say.

They all ate a dinner of the abundant turkey leftovers in the breakfast nook. Mandy had the feeling the dining table wasn't used for meals so much as it served as a buffet table when company came. After they cleared the dinner dishes, Jake's parents vanished up the stairs for the old, familiar ritual of last-minute gift wrapping.

"Should we put out a plate for Santa now?" Emily asked.

She was looking at Jake. Mandy waited to hear what he'd say.

"It's a little early, but it couldn't hurt," he said. "Right?"

He locked his gaze with Mandy's. Her heart kicked up. "Absolutely," she said.

Once again, there was something unspoken in his look, but Mandy didn't want to try to guess at its meaning. She'd been wrong too many times already. Instead, she took Emily to the kitchen and found a plate for the cookies. They walked back out to the living room with Emily bearing the cookies, while Mandy carried a glass of milk.

"Where should they go?" Emily asked.

Jake cleared a space on one of the two lamp tables flanking the sofa, the one that was closest to the fireplace. "Here," he said. "This is where I always put them." He took the plate and glass and set them down. "The trick is to keep Grandpa from eating them."

At Emily's concerned look, Mandy said, "Don't worry. We'll keep an eye on it. If he eats any, we'll put more out after he goes to bed."

Now she and Jake stood on opposite sides of the little end table, a plate of cookies between them. Time seemed to slow. Mandy was aware of Jake's parents coming back down the stairs, discussing which Christmas movie to watch; Emily, looking at the plate of cookies with a mixture of anticipation and hope; but most of all, Jake's eyes, and some unspoken intent there.

"Let's go outside for a minute," he said.

Mandy nodded.

As Jake went to the closet for their jackets, she remembered the night they'd talked on her front porch. *Jake's revenge,* she thought as she stepped outside into the biting cold. Then she stood entranced as the winter night greeted her. White icicle lights hung from the eaves above her head, and in the sky beyond, the stars were brilliant. It hadn't snowed since their arrival, but a sparkling crust still covered the lawn. Mandy tried to slow her breathing so she could hear it: that Christmas Eve stillness, the quiet pause of expectation.

She felt Jake's hand on her elbow, and the warmth from his touch seemed to spread up her arm to ward off the chill. She pulled in a big breath of the cold air. Time to face him.

She turned. "Jake, I'm sorry. I—"

"Don't." He pulled her nearer, resting his forehead against hers. "I almost blew it with Emily. You were right. Sometimes it's hard for a guy like me to understand about things like . . . magic."

"What did you tell her?"

"Pretty much the same thing your mother told you about Santa. That he's the spirit of Christmas. But I didn't bring you out here to talk about Emily."

Her heart sped up.

"Look." He clasped his arms around her waist,

holding her loosely to look down into her face. "Do I believe there's a white-haired guy who's going to come down the chimney tonight? No. But it's important to believe in something, and I don't ever want to take that away from anyone. Not Emily, not you. Not me, either. And I believe in Mandy Reese."

"And I believe in you," she said. "Whether you agree with me on everything or not."

"That's good, because I need you. A guy can't be rational all the time. You cut through all the pluses and minuses. You make me remember what's important. Whatever happened with you, whatever you saw that night all those years ago—I don't know what it was. But you've got something nobody else has. And I don't want to live without it."

He brushed a strand of hair away from her face. "The thing is, I don't like moving forward without a plan. I think I can make this Christmas hotel work. But it's risky. It may not be entirely . . . practical."

A smile tugged at her lips. "You know how much I hate that word."

"Right. But I couldn't jump into something like this without you. *That* would be crazy. So . . ." Jake looked up at the deepening blue of the night. He'd planned for this moment, gotten it off to a false start, and now that it was here, he wasn't sure what to say. "Is it too early for a Christmas present? I've been carrying this one around for a while."

Everything in her face encouraged him, but his fingers still shook as he reached into his coat pocket to bring out the little red velvet box. It had picked up some lint over the past few days, and he brushed at it. The cold made his fingers clumsy as he pried open the box and turned the ring toward Mandy. The Christmas lights from the eaves did their part to set the cluster of small diamonds sparkling. He heard her draw in a soft breath.

Finally he knew exactly what to say. "Mandy, will you marry me?"

"Yes," she said, and he was gratified to feel her arms around his neck, to be able to bury his face in the softness of her hair. She fit against him, giving him warmth.

"Hey," his tongue-tied mouth said. "You're supposed to let me put the ring on first."

He kissed her, still clutching the box. It was a few more minutes before he put the ring on her finger.

Afterward, Jake rested his cheek on the top of her head, and they looked up at the night sky together. "We'd better go inside," Jake said. "Time to celebrate Christmas Eve with the family."

"Wait." Mandy pointed up at a tiny red light crossing the sky. "Do you see what I see?"

Jake wasn't sure if she was kidding or not, but he took a chance. He'd been honest with her up to this point; now wasn't the time to start pulling punches. "It's an airplane, Mandy."

She considered it for a moment, then nodded. "You're right. It's too early for Santa."


Okay, he felt like a kid at Christmas.

Jake couldn't sleep, and he was tired of grinning at the ceiling like an idiot. So he tiptoed down the stairs for a snack. Anyway, since he was embracing all this, it might not be a bad idea if some of those cookies got eaten.

The house felt so silent, every step Jake took on the stairs sounded magnified to his ears. He thought of the line Mandy had quoted: *Not a creature was stirring . . .*

The dim light from the entrance hall guided him. Beyond that, through the arched doorway to the living room, he could make out the soft glow from the Christmas tree, its lights left on overnight in honor of the holiday.

The closer he got to the room, the slower and more careful his steps got. After all this, it really wouldn't do to get caught eating Santa's cookies.

When he reached the living room archway, he heard a child's voice whispering. It had to be Emily. But who was she talking to?

He peered into the room. On the far wall, he saw a large shadow cast by the light of the Christmas tree. If he didn't know better, he would have sworn he recognized the shape of a man dressed in a very distinctive suit, the same figure he'd seen on a thousand Christmas cards.

Then, for an instant, he couldn't see anything at all as a brilliant flash of light filled the room.

Jake blinked and waited for his vision to clear. When it did, the room was dim again, illuminated only by the Christmas tree. The shadow on the wall was gone.

And Emily was peering up the chimney.